The Lake Point Deeps

By Peter Redmond

ISBN: 978-1-7327163-2-2 (Paperback Edition)

ISBN: 978-1-7327163-3-9 (Electronic Edition)

Editing by Dustin Bilyk

Front Cover Image by Michael Landon

Published by AB Publishing

This book is dedicated to my children.

I love you with all that I am.

I would like to thank my parents for showing me that anything is possible.

I owe a great debt of gratitude to Michelle Redmond and Kathy Redmond. Both suffered through my earlier drafts and kept me motivated with their tireless encouragement. Thank you.

CHAPTER 1

Sitting on damp pine needles, Michelle could feel cool wetness seeping through her shorts as her bad leg throbbed with each heartbcat. Her protective Ogre remained motionless, doing its best to hide its massive bulk despite the flurry of battle noises coming from where Peter was storming the dam.

She needed to be able to see the trail to stop Billy and Judd when they came with help, but she also needed to stay hidden in case some monsters came looking for them, so she found a place for the Ogre to lay down among some taller bushes. As long as you didn't look directly where it was, and it continued to stay still, she hoped it would be difficult to spot. She listened to the sounds of battle in the distance.

She glanced down at her digital watch again. It had been nearly five minutes since the battle started. She didn't know what she expected, but it seemed like it was taking a lot longer than it should have. She craned her neck a bit to see if any water had come down the muddy streambed. Nothing. That meant the dam was still intact.

Torturing herself, she imagined what it would mean if she heard the fighting stop and there was no water rushing in from the broken dam. If that happened, she would wait, motionless and hidden in the woods, waiting for Peter to return. But how many hours would pass before she would admit what had happened? What would she do?

It would mean that . . . she didn't want to think about what it would mean. But it might happen. She had learned at a very early age that bad things do happen to good people.

Michelle had essentially been an only child growing up, for it wasn't until middle-school that she gained the first of her two eventual brothers. When she was in elementary school, she could remember waiting up with her mother for her father to come home. He worked long hours in a factory and rarely came home before she went to bed, but that was just fine with her. If it was her bedtime before he got home, it meant that she could sleep with her mom in their bed, which at that age was like winning the lottery.

They lived in a comfortable house and life was good. She had a backyard with plenty of green grass and one of those metal blister-inducing jungle gyms that everyone had back then. Hot summer days were spent lounging in the above-ground pool that took up two thirds of the back yard, and the winter was spent alternating between tall lopsided snowmen and steaming warm, Swiss Miss hot chocolate with the pebble-sized, freeze-dried marshmallows. Life was comfortable and good.

Then one day her father hurt his back at work. He was barely able to stand. The factory said that if he couldn't do his job that they would have to let him go. It was okay though, her mom had said. He was hurt at work, so he would be paid for it. But then something happened.

There were court dates and dealings behind closed doors. In the end, the factory didn't pay for anything, not even the medical bills. Their world changed. They talked about moving and selling things. Her mother went to work, and her father had to stop going to the doctor's office. Michelle could tell that her daddy's back still hurt, but he had to choose between keeping their home or go to the doctors. Nothing was guaranteed anymore.

It was as if she had been happily playing hopscotch only to look down and realize that she was standing on thin glass over a dark abyss. Terrified and motionless, she could hear the snapping of hairline cracks under her feet as she waited for the support to give way and plunge her down into darkness. Now she knew that everything had been supported by the thinnest most fragile of barriers, and it terrified her. There was no safety net, no one to come to rescue them.

They didn't fall though. Her mother continued to support them until her father was able recover and work through the pain. After many years of long and grueling hours, he became a successful business owner. The thin, cracked glass that they had once stood upon had become thick and solid as marble. They regained their comfortable life twice over and then had two more children who grew up unaware of how close the family had come to falling.

But Michelle knew. She had glimpsed at what lay below. She had seen that below the apparent solidity of routine awaits the dark chasm of an unexpected fall, ready to swallow up the fragile happiness of life. Since then, she'd never looked down to see the thin glass cracking beneath her feet, but she knew how the real world worked.

Now, as she sat on the damp ground with her leg broken, hearing her husband battle for everyone's survival and her children soon to enter into an unknown world of danger, she dared not look down.

A flash of red movement from the trail caught her eye. She held her breath and leaned to one side to get a better look. She couldn't tell exactly who it was, but she could tell from their cautious movements that they were human, and they were looking for someone.

Michelle thought about yelling but decided that it was a bad idea. Despite the noise coming from upstream, she didn't feel like giving her position away to everyone and everything within earshot. She struggled to one leg and began waving at the figure on the trail. The figure saw her movement and had sense enough to not call out in acknowledgement. Instead, they waved back.

Michelle stood on her one leg in silence as the figure jogged over to her. "Billy!" Michelle shouted in whisper.

"Hi there," he said, nodding to her knee. "You okay?"

Michelle gave him the same inventory-taking review. His blue shirt was soaked with dark wetness, and while she wasn't sure if it was sweat or blood, he was visibly banged up in a few places but seemed to well enough to walk.

"I think I broke my leg," she said, but then regretted taking any of his attention away from the task at hand. She gestured toward the dam. "Peter and one of the Ogres are upstream. The bad guys built a dam and the water can contain them if we destroy the dam."

"Right," said Billy, clearly not understanding anything but trusting her anyway. He'd seen the Ogres, Elves and, if the guts on his left shoulder meant anything, some big bugs as well. "Peter left you alone like this?"

Michelle pointed over her shoulder to where the blind Ogre lay hidden. Billy's eyebrows raised in acknowledgement. As she filled him in further, Michelle saw a small crowd gathering on the trail where Billy had stopped.

"You all need to hurry. We need to break the dam. If too many monsters cross before we get the water flowing, the old man said the barrier will stop working altogether."

"Can't be havin' that now, can we?" Billy said, winking at her. He ran back to the trail and exchanged some words with the group. By the way he gestured it looked like he was splitting them in two. Michelle wanted to join, but she could only wait.

"Hi, sunshine!" said a voice behind her.

"Jenn?" asked Michelle, trying to turn her head and see who it was.

"None other!"

"Where are the kids?" asked Michelle.

"Don't worry. They're with us," she said, gesturing back to the trail. "Think I would leave the munchkins all on their own with those nasties flying about?"

"Jenn, it's dangerous here. That's why we left them at your house. The woods are crawling with monsters," Michelle said, then remembered. "Where is William?"

Before she finished the sentence, a little body came rumbling down the trail. Michelle could see that both hands were clutched, holding toys. One held a matchbox die cast car in one hand and she couldn't see what was in the other. This was an automatic unconscious observation that Michelle made whenever one of her children was running, which was grouped with the general assessment of how much damage should be expected in the event of a fall.

A running two-year-old child with full hands meant that if he fell, he would not drop what he was holding to catch himself. Instead, he would hold onto what he had, and either skin his knuckles by using his clenched fists to slow his descent or throw his hands wide in the tactic of landing belly first which almost always resulted in a bumped chin. Other important factors influencing the fall to no-fall ratio was terrain evenness (ranging from nice flat grass to death trap uneven sidewalk), child age, how tired the child was (which seemed to be the main factor defining how high they raised their feet when running), shoes or no shoes, and child happiness level. For some reason the happier the child the greater chance of them falling. A tired and happy child running full tilt barefoot on an uneven sidewalk in shorts and a t-shirt with full hands is the equivalent of a Defcon-1 Nuclear Alert. Now watching William sprinting to her on the uneven, hard-packed dirt path, Michelle made the appropriate inner cringe in acknowledgement of his likely fall.

And of course, less than halfway to her, his foot caught on a root and he tumbled. He made the questionable choice of the arms-splayed-wide maneuver, which was a good choice for flat asphalt or concrete, but less beneficial on the uneven, root-laden trail surface. Jenn and Michelle let out an "augh!" as his stomach hit a fraction of a second before his head. The unevenness of the trail prevented his stomach from absorbing most of the momentum before his head snapped forward and impacted a poorly-placed gnarled root.

Despite her bad leg, she started limping to him, already shushing what was to be an epic wailing session. To her surprise, he popped back up and bounced the remaining few feet to her still smiling and saying "Mommy, Mommy!"

She lifted him up checked his face where he had hit the root and found nothing, not even a red mark. She checked his legs and stomach too, soliciting a giggle from William.

"Yeah, about that . . ." started Jenn.

Michelle's stomach sank remembering she hadn't identified what was in his left hand. She pulled his hand close and saw a dark black stone between his thick, meaty fingers.

"How did he get that?" she asked.

"I don't know," said Jenn. "He was playing trains one second and then suddenly he was throwing cars like a Major League Baseball pitcher. I think it makes him stronger. A LOT stronger."

Michelle remembered the Screecher that had produced this stone. It had been half the size of a house and nearly impossible to kill. The sheer mass of the thing had made it impossible to overpower. They had to pin it with Peter's car and then light it on fire, and that almost wasn't even enough.

She remembered how Shannon had nearly died when she first used her stone. Peter's stone created a twin that tried the steal the stone from him. Even Michelle's stone would slow her down and make her weak if she wasn't careful about her thoughts. These stones were too dangerous for anyone, let alone a barely two-year-old boy.

"Will-Will. Give Mommy the stone," she said holding out her hand.

"Mines," he said with an eyes-closed head shake.

"William. Give it to Mommy."

"No! Mines."

Michelle grabbed the stone from his hand. Well, at least that was what she intended to do. His fingers were like thick metal bands. She tried again, working her hand around his pinky finger and pulling hard to break his grip. Nothing. She couldn't move it an inch.

She noticed that William was watching this with semi-detached interest. It was apparent that he knew there was no way she was going to get the stone without his consent.

He looked at her and said, "Mines," adding a nod for emphasis.

Michelle gave up and instead settled for a snuggle. William hugged back. She realized after the embrace that she should have been concerned that he might have squeezed the breakfast out of her, but thankfully, it was a normal snuggle.

CHAPTER 2

"Jenn, it's not safe here. Peter is fighting a bunch of armed Orcs a few-hundred feet from here, and the forest is overrun with monsters," Michelle said. "What were you thinking?"

"So is the neighborhood, Michelle. And, as far as we know, so is the rest of the county," Jenn said, then continued in a lower voice. "We got attacked. Erin got hurt pretty bad. Don't ask her about . . ."

"What are we not talking about?" asked Erin walking up from the trail.

She was holding her youngest, and behind her was a trail of children that reminded Michelle of little ducklings, probably because Erin was looking especially rubber ducky. It looked like she had done one of those new-age Color Runs and the organizers only hit her with yellow paint. Her hair was matted down against her head as if over-loaded with too much hair spray, and she wore bright, clean elbow-length white gloves that seemed to have somehow avoided the abuse the rest of her had sustained.

"Um . . . hi, Erin!" said Michelle, trying not to laugh.

Discrete as ever, Jenn slid behind Erin, made wide eyes at Michelle and shook her head. She pointed to one of her hands.

"You're, uh, looking especially yellow today." Michelle said, making sure not to mention the forbidden white glove question.

"Yeah, sure, thanks," said Erin, pointing down at Michelle with one of her white gloves. "How's the leg?"

"I can't put weight on it. Peter thinks it is a dislocated kneecap. It might be broken too," she replied.

Jenn's nursing instincts kicked in and she dropped down to poke at Michelle's knee. "Definitely dislocated," she said. "There isn't any way to tell for sure if it is broken without an x-ray. No bone is sticking through the skin so at least there is that."

Billy and ten others came over to Michelle. "Where are they, exactly?"

"Follow the stream, Billy. It shouldn't be too far. You can hear it," she said, ushering them toward the dam. "Hurry, would you? They've been fighting for a while."

"Do they have an Ogre?"

"Yes," said Michelle. "Just the one."

"Then we'll take one more with us and leave the other two here for you and the kids," he said, tilting his head back to the trail.

Billy and the ten others started walking upstream with an Ogre in tow. Michelle didn't recognize any of them. Most of them had guns and all of them had some medieval looking weapon. One or two had long spears that she remembered were called pikes. She saw a few axes, not the wood cutting kind, but real double-edged battle axes. The rest had an assortment of blades, ranging from double knives all the way up to two-handed long swords.

Michelle turned back to see another group of at least thirty more people coming down the trail.

"Where did you get all these people and where did they get the weapons? Did I see a spiked mace?" Michelle asked.

Jenn smiled "Bryan. Who knew?"

"What do you mean "Bryan"?"

"Apparently he and Marci are renaissance fair freaks. They have a whole armory set up in their basement," said Jenn. "Good thing, too."

Michelle was able to pick Judd out of the crew by his height. She couldn't see Bryan or Marci.

"What about the other people?" she asked again. "I don't recognize any of them."

"Apparently Bryan and Marci know half of the neighborhood," said Erin.

"How many people?" asked Michelle.

"I'm not one-hundred percent sure but it's gotta be close to thirty," said Jenn, shrugging her shoulders.

Michelle could see that they were settling in on the main trail. She could see them corralling the kids into the center of a circle made of up heavily armed men and women.

"Where are your Ogres?" asked Michelle.

"You know, I'm not sure," said Erin. "We should join the rest of the group."

Michelle called out to the Ogre in a semi-hushed shout. "Hey, big guy. You should probably stay where you are. There are too many of us small people to step on. If we need your help, you'll likely hear it. We'll be on the trail."

The hidden mountain of a beast blew air out of his nose in acknowledgement, kicking up a cloud of leaves and sticks. Jenn leaned in to take William from Michelle so that she could hobble to the group, but William put up a fuss and held on tight to Michelle. Instead, Jenn lent a shoulder to Michelle and they played caboose to Erin's small train of children.

Now with the group, she saw some familiar faces. Bryan was organizing the group's arrangement for optimal defense. He had on a chain mail shirt that fell down to about mid-thigh with thick sturdy leather belt pulling in the slack of his armor. Hung from the belt were two curved scabbards. He gave a wide smile when he noticed Michelle had joined the group.

"Hi Michelle!" he called. "Messed up your knee, eh?"

"Yeah," she replied. "Nice armor. Renaissance fairs? Really?"

"Oh, yeah!" replied Bryan. "That's how Marci and I met. We both love it."

He gestured down to his suit. "We collect a lot of reproductions from different periods. Some of it isn't very functional, you know, looks good but wouldn't last a second in a real fight. But, as you can see, a lot of it is going to get good use today!" he said with his arms wide, looking back at his group of self-made warriors.

Marci walked over, wearing a leather vest over a blue, quick-dry t-shirt. She had what looked like two small hatchets in her hands and Michelle noted a few knife sheaths strategically secured around her body. Michelle could see by the lack of luster on the hatchets they had been used.

"Did you meet any bad guys?" asked Michelle.

"I hate bugs," commented Marci.

"Yeah" said Bryan. "After Judd and Billy told us what was going on and we gathered a rescue party, we had to fight our way through an army of centipedes to get to his house. We came just in the nick of time."

"Don't ask Erin about the gloves," said Marci in a low tone.

"Why? What is . . ." began Michelle, but before she could finish someone came running from the other side of the bridge.

"Jack, what did you see?" asked Bryan.

Jack looked to be in his mid-thirties and relatively athletic. He was panting as he tried to speak. "Too many. Too many. We need to leave now!"

"Jack, take a breath. What is it? Too many what?" asked Bryan, grabbing him by his shoulders, trying to calm him.

"I – I don't know what they were. They looked like small green children, but with knives. Big, rusty knives!" answered Jack. "And something big . . . Something *really* big was coming. I didn't wait. We need to go now!"

"Goblins. They are Goblins," said Michelle. "How many?"

"I don't know. More than a hundred," he said. "I couldn't see them all. I had to leave or they would have seen me. But they are coming this way and there was something behind them. I didn't see it, but trees were falling before and around it. It must have been huge."

"Could be more centipedes cutting trees," said Michelle.

"No. The trees didn't fall like that. They weren't cut! They were pushed out of the way by something big, snapping like bamboo. We need to go. This isn't the place to fight them. We will be surrounded. We need to go," said Jack, trying to get his breath. He was terrified.

If they're coming this way, then that must mean . . .

Bryan pressed his lips together, thinking about what to do. Michelle stepped forward. "They can't cross moving water. The stream is dry right now. We just need to break the dam so the water starts flowing."

"Okay," said Bryan, scratching behind his ear. "So we break the dam and then get the heck out of here."

"No," answered Michelle. "They might still be able to cross the bridges, though it's supposed to be difficult for them. And they could also build another dam."

Jack wasn't satisfied. "Look. My wife and kids are here. I thought we were going to help round up a few bad actors. What are we going to do if the dam doesn't break? We can't risk it. We need to go!"

He walked into the crowd and joined his wife. She was holding what looked to be a one-year-old baby. Michelle could see that he was talking to her about where to go.

Michelle spoke up. "Billy just took a group to help Peter break the dam. Once the water flows, we only need to guard the bridges and make sure they don't build any more dams. If we don't, there will be nothing to stop more of them from crossing and it won't matter where we go."

Jack turned from his conversation with his wife. "What do we care if a couple-hundred Goblins make it out? We can jump in a car and be a hundred miles from here in a few –"

"It won't be a couple-hundred! If too many cross the barrier, then it fails. That means they can *all* cross. Not just a few, Jack. Millions and millions of terrors. And the ones we've seen are just the warm up, the ones that stay close to the surface. Do you know why they stay close to the surface? Because the ones down in the deeps scare *them.*" She paused to let that sink in. She was starting to sound like the old man.

"We need to wait. When the dam is broken, it doesn't matter how many of them there are. They can only try to cross the bridge a few at a time. We can handle that. And the Ogres will make sure they don't set up any more dams." As she finished she realized she had been shouting.

Her free hand was shaking. If they left, she would be giving up on Shannon, Arthur and Caitlin. Their trek into the cave would be pointless. The barrier would be broken and everywhere would already be overrun with monsters. She couldn't let that happen.

Someone shouted. They all looked across the bridge to see Goblins advancing through the woods. They were spread out as far in either direction as Michelle could see. She wasn't able to see very far into the woods, so she could only see a few rows deep, but from the sound of their advance she would not have been surprised if the formation was as deep as it was wide.

The Goblins were not marching in any discernible cadence, but the advancing lines were maintaining form and distance, if not rhythmic footfalls. Michelle could see why Jack wanted to leave.

They wouldn't need to be surrounded. The sheer volume of Goblins could rush and trample the thirty-member group. They wouldn't stand a chance without the river flowing.

Michelle watched as Bryan, Judd, Jenn and Marci ran around the group, organizing their defense. They moved everyone closer to the bridges, to a point where the trail passed through a thick copse of trees, providing them some limited protection from both sides. Two Ogres took up positions in the front and the remaining guarded the rear. Michelle shuffled over to the front of the makeshift wall where she could better see the stream.

Still no water.

Michelle listened for the sound of battle in the distance, but even if there was any, the approaching Goblin horde muffled it completely.

The first line of Goblins made it to the bridges, and just like when the Ogres first tried to cross, they leaned into the bridge as if a strong headwind was pushing them back. Unlike the Ogres, however, they couldn't get within thirty feet or so of the bridge before it would send them flying backwards. Despite everything that was going on, Michelle allowed herself to smile at the small green figures being catapulted back into their ranks, causing Goblins to topple like bowling pins.

The following ranks, however, did not stop their march forward. Soon the front rank was pushed into the muddy streambed, facedown, and the Goblins' hesitation was replaced with surprise when they were able to step through and even cross the streambed unmolested. The mass of troops redirected from the bridges and walked over their fallen comrades from one bank to the other. The first few Goblins were now close enough for Michelle to see their dark, stained toothy grins.

For the briefest of moments, Michelle shut her eyes, grabbed her stone and wished with all that she knew that timing would be in her favor. They needed the dam broken and they needed it broken now. Life wasn't always fair, but she needed this. They all needed this.

She let go of her stone and opened her eyes. At first, she thought it was her imagination, but when she saw the first trickle of water rushing down the streambed she knew it was real. It wasn't a lot of water, only a foot or two high, but when it came rushing down the stream bed it was as if a freight train had hit the Goblins. Those within ten feet of either side of the stream exploded into the air, catapulting above and beyond the tops of the tall old growth pine trees.

Those in the stream didn't fare nearly as well. They ceased to be.

One second they were there, and the next they were gone. What struck Michelle most about the scene was the lack of sound. She could hear the flowing water and the Goblin's shrieks of surprise and pain, but no sound accompanied the invisible force that shot them up into the air or vaporized them instantly.

The small band, who had been preparing to be completely overrun, gave a rousing cheer. Even the little kids joined in the fun, clapping their little hands together and jumping around in small circles. Michelle allowed herself a smile. She could almost hear Peter saying something like "come on, have a little faith!" or "of course it would work out. It's me!"

Through the cheer, Michelle heard an Ogre barking from downstream where the dam had broken. She hadn't spent much time with the Ogres, but she could tell this was not good news. She saw the Ogres just in front of her processing the communication and, without knowing why, she looked at the stream again.

She couldn't tell for sure, but the water didn't seem as deep as she remembered. The Ogre to the right of her turned its large head to face her. It shook its head. She looked again at the stream. This time she was sure the water was shallower, and now it didn't look like it was moving at all.

The Goblins on the other side also noticed how the water had stopped flowing. They started creeping closer, testing their way. On her side of the stream, Michelle heard something running through the woods and turned to see one of Billy's men.

"Another dam!" he shouted. "There was another dam behind the one we broke!"

No . . . This isn't fair . . . We don't have enough time!

The Goblins edged closer to the stagnant muddy water. There would probably be another dam behind the next one, and maybe another one after that, and it was just a matter of time before the Goblins discovered they could cross. There just wasn't time.

She heard a familiar voice shouting to the group, "This is our last chance to go! We tried. They broke the dam and it didn't work. There isn't any use in us getting killed out here!"

It was Jack. And, this time, he was right.

Michelle didn't need to look where she stood. She had already felt her own dam break. She was falling into a black nothingness and no one was going to save her.

CHAPTER 3

Michelle sank down to the ground. Around her, everyone was a flurry of activity. Jack was continuing his calls for a retreat. Bryan and Judd were talking with the runner who came from the dams, discussing the coordination of their retreat so they wouldn't leave behind Billy, Peter and the others behind. All three Ogres were between the humans and the Goblin horde approaching the stagnant stream with intense scrutiny of what might be happening upstream.

"We need to go now! Now!" Jack was yelling to the group.

He and his wife and child were already down the trail as far away from the stream as possible without leaving the group. It was clear that he very much wanted to flee in the safety of numbers. As for Michelle, she sat behind the Ogres, throwing away any chance she would have of seeing Shannon, Arthur and Caitlin. Without holding the line now, everything would be lost. Too many would cross the barrier, breaking it. It wasn't fair. Life just wasn't fair, and her entire family was in the middle of it.

She could almost hear the old man's voice from their conversation in the basement yesterday. "Expecting life to be fair because you are a fair and good person is like expecting a lion not to eat you because you chose not to eat it."

***

It seemed like years ago when the old man had taken each of the Redmond family down to the basement one by one to reveal the secrets of their stones. Michelle remembered sitting in the living room with her kids; William in her lap safe from the monstrous bat that had almost taken him, and Shannon, Arthur and Caitlin huddling in close together on the couch.

Michelle heard the characteristic creak of the basement door. Peter walked into the living room with a pensive look.

"Your turn," Peter said, pointing to Michelle.

"My turn? What did he say to you?" asked Michelle.

"I would love to tell you if I could figure it out myself. I'll let you know when I do."

Michelle passed a protesting William to Peter and went down into the basement. On her way down the stairs she heard a rhythmic noise she knew well.

"Peter said you wanted to talk to me," called Michelle over the sound of the old man bouncing on the trampoline they'd put in the basement for rainy days. It was just large enough for all four kids to use at the same time, but small enough to fit within the basement's standard-height ceiling.

"Correct!" called the old man through the protective screen mesh surrounding the trampoline. Enjoying himself, he began to bounce in rapid, little circles.

Michelle watched for about thirty seconds before saying, "You said that you were going to tell us about the secrets of our stones?"

The old man shifted from bouncing on one foot to the other. He was having a hard time at it and fell once or twice. Each fall was punctuated with what sounded like a soft curse under his breath, but as he got up, she could see a smile on his face. This was the man they were going to let take their kids into some cave? He was clearly insane.

"Well . . .?" said Michelle. The old man just giggled. "Are you crazy?" asked Michelle.

The old man stopped bouncing and considered the question. Even though his body was still, the trampoline continued to rock his body up and down like a man on a boat in choppy seas.

"Sometimes I wonder at that," said the old man. "It would be a very worrying thing to lose."

"Your mind?" asked Michelle.

"No, my crazy!" replied the old man with another giggle. He started jumping again, sending out occasional whoops to punctuate certain bounces.

"If you're just going to play around and not tell me about my stone, I might as well –"

"Aren't I?"

"Aren't you what?" asked Michelle, annoyed.

The old man looked at her for a second or two, then threw his hands up in the air and started bouncing again.

"There isn't time for this. You were the one who said there isn't time," said Michelle.

"Exactly!" replied the old man with a large bounce.

"Exactly what?" asked Michelle. "Never mind. This isn't going anywhere. I already know what my stone does. I used it to get William back from the bat."

"Oh? Do tell!"

"When I held it, if I thought good things it would get hot and I would gain ability. Like if I told myself I was fast, I got faster. But if I was thinking bad thoughts, it would get cold and it would hurt me. Like if I focused on how tired I was, I felt a lot more tired," explained Michelle.

"Good! Good!" said the old man. "But not everything."

"So? Tell me more."

"Telling, everyone wants telling," said the old man. "Come closer." He stopped jumping and walked to the edge of the trampoline.

Michelle came closer and matched his serious gaze through the mesh netting. The old man leaned in so that his nose pushed up against it. "Listen carefully for the wisdom of what I am about to show you, for it may very well save your life one day," he said in a low serious tone. Michelle nodded, and the old man continued, serious as ever, "Never ask a two-year-old to hold a tomato." He threw his little body back, flopping into the center of the trampoline and rolled with laughter.

"What?" asked Michelle, smiling despite her best efforts.

The old man looked up at her and seemed delighted to see her smile. "Yes! You see? You see now?" She shrugged, not understanding. "Here. We will do it once again." He pulled himself up and rushed over to the screen mesh, pushing his nose up against it.

This time he had a hard time holding the seriousness in his voice. She could tell his will-power was fighting a losing battle against the smiles laying siege to his face. Michelle couldn't help but smile in return.

"Never! Never-ever let your mother brush your hair when she is mad at your father," he said with a quick wink at the end. Once again, he fell into a heap of laughter in the center of the trampoline.

This time Michelle's face broke into an unrestrained smile and she even laughed a bit. The old man caught her laughter and sat up, pointing. "You see? You see? Now I have shown you the secret of your stone."

Michelle spoke through her smile, "You've shown me that you can make me laugh. *That's* the secret of my stone?"

"Yes! Just so!" said the old man standing up proudly.

Michelle paused to consider what he was saying. "You suffer from insanity," she said under her breath.

"Quite the contrary," said the old man, beaming. "I very much enjoy it."

"I really don't understand what you are trying to tell me," she said, smile vanishing. "I need to be able to help my children."

"Not tell, show. Telling is easy. The mind is so quick to decide. And words do not convince the soul."

"Fine. I need to know," she said.

"No, you don't. You need to feel," said the old man. "That is the secret of the stone."

"Humor me."

The old man smiled wide again, mumbling something to himself that sounded like it started with "stubborn, old . . ." but she couldn't quite hear.

"Close your eyes," he requested.

Michelle raised an eyebrow to which, in turn, he raised both back. She conceded and closed her eyes. She listened.

"Imagine it is winter. It is cold, and you are outside. The snow is thick all around you. You feel the cold wind on your face. Tell me what you see and how you feel."

"It is dark and cold. There are trees but no leaves. They are all spindly and dead-looking. I'm cold. My fingers are going numb.

I want to be inside before my toes go numb. It is dangerous to be out in the cold for too long," she said. Since she was a child, she'd always had a vivid imagination, an almost uncanny ability to put herself in any situation.

The old man sighed.

"What?" asked Michelle, opening her eyes.

"Winter is unavoidable. It is part of life," said the old man in a serious tone.

"I know. It comes right after fall," said Michelle. "It's fun for about two weeks and then I wish it was spring again."

The old man bounce-walked over to the opening in the mesh cover and climbed down from the trampoline. He came over to stand just in front of her. Standing this close, she reconsidered him. He was very small for an adult, only coming up to about her waist. His dark-brown robe looked like it had been reassembled more than a few times. In fact, it looked like it should have been thrown away more than a decade ago. Both his hair and beard were stark white and looked as if they'd never been combed. His dark brown eyes sparkled as they looked up at her. She realized then that she knew him. She didn't know who he was, but she did know him.

"Who are you?" she asked.

The old man's mouth moved as if he was going to say something but then shut again. He looked away briefly before saying, "In life it will rain. We cannot stop the rain. That is not our choice. What is left for us is to decide what we do in the rain. Some will choose to run from it, others will choose to curse the sky, and others will learn to dance in it. None are right, and none are wrong. It is everyone's choice to make."

Michelle responded unimpressed. "Yeah, I got that. My stone responds to happy thoughts and negative thoughts. This isn't anything new."

"No, not just the stone," the old man said softly. "Much more than the stone."

"What do you mean? Quit being so cryptic."

"Our minds are not simple observers. They are also projectors," he replied. "Our beliefs and intentions create the world around us."

"Are you telling me *we* caused these monsters to attack us?"

"No. Nothing like that. The world contains, in every second, both the most hellish atrocities imaginable and the most wondrously beautiful miracles conceivable. We choose how to live within those conflicting opposites. We can either choose to live our dreams or choose to live our nightmares. Both are equally offered. It is up to us which to choose."

"I didn't choose to be attacked by monsters," Michelle said.

"No. You didn't," he admitted. "Yet they are not here, and still even now you allow them to continue to injure you. The enemy does not need to bind your arms. If he can tie up your mind, he has already won."

"So I'm supposed to be happy that my family is being attacked by monsters? Am I supposed to ignore them? That doesn't make any sense."

"You must do what is necessary and choose to live your dreams or your fears," he said.

"I don't see how any of this could be considered a dream," she said. "Peter was right. None of this makes any sense."

"Right now, there is someone sitting in a hospital wishing they had the same chance you do," said the old man.

"To do what . . . fight for their life?" asked Michelle.

"No. To fight for their child's," replied the old man.

Michelle paused, the words extending roots into her consciousness, but they found no purchase in her tired state. It was late, so much had happened that day, and old man was wasting her time with empty words. She began walking up the stairs.

"In the winter," the old man called up to her as she walked up the stairs, "I enjoy sledding. And snow is really just unassembled snowmen."

He's crazy.

***

"Let's go, Let's go!" yelled Jack, bringing Michelle out of her musings.

She shook her head and smiled a bit to herself. She understood now. She had work to do. If only she could make it start raining, then it wouldn't even matter if there were one-hundred dams – the river would flow. The idea hit her so suddenly that she gasped for air.

"Oh, they are going to love this one," she giggled to herself.

"Bryan!" she called over to get his attention before he let the runner go back to Peter and Billy.

It took her a minute to get to her feet, but she wanted to stand. She fished the stone out of her pocket and spoke with him. She could feel its warm feedback as she described what the runner needed to say to the second group by the dams. Bryan listened and nodded.

"Michelle, I trust you, but why do you want them to do that? It doesn't make sense," he said.

"I know. It will in a minute, but the runner needs to go now. I'll explain everything. It's our only chance, Bryan."

Bryan nodded and ran over to the runner to relay the information. Michelle waved over Jenn who was trying to help corral the children.

"What?" Jenn asked. "Are we leaving?"

"No. Put my kneecap back."

"Um. I might be able to do that, but if your leg is broken it isn't going to help," said Jenn.

"I know. Do it."

"It is going to hurt. A lot."

"Jenn, I had four children without any pain killers. Do it," said Michelle.

"Okay, keep your leg straight as you can and don't jerk it around. Keep still. Put your hands on my shoulders so that you don't fall. This is going to hurt." Jenn knelt to get a better angle on her knee.

Michelle looked away to the stream. Kamikaze suicidal as they were, it seemed that the Goblins weren't excited about trying to cross the stream again. That was good. They needed some extra time. Then something tore her leg off from the knee. At least that is what it felt like.

"Ooooowww!" shouted Michelle. "That hurt!"

"I said it would," said Jenn. "Try it."

Michelle looked down at her purplish green knee. Now at least the general form was something that could be squinted at and considered a proper knee shape. She put some weight on it. It hurt, but not like before. She put more weight on it and it hurt a lot more, but at least it seemed to be holding her up.

"If you can do that, it probably isn't a compound fracture," said Jenn. "But that doesn't mean you don't have a hairline fracture somewhere in there."

"Thanks, Jenn," said Michelle.

They walked to the middle of the group. Michelle still held her stone and willed herself to walk as much as possible without a limp.

"Everyone!" she called out, "I know what we need to do to save our children and ourselves and to keep those things from our world! Come closer. I don't want to risk our enemies hearing."

"For goodness sake!" shouted Jack "There isn't time! We need to go, now! They could cross any minute!"

"Then go. It's your choice. And no one will try to stop you. But you all need to know that this is our last chance to keep this evil from spreading into the world," she said to everyone.

"So you will die here?" asked Jack. "For what? If we get to a car we could all be two states away before night falls."

"We need to end it here and now," answered Michelle. "There are more of these things than there are of us. If we let them out now they will take over and there won't be anywhere to hide."

"You don't know that. I want to live. I want to stay alive today," said Jack, grabbing his child from his wife.

He was now joined by at least eight other people.

Michelle felt the rock heating up in her hand. She wasn't sure if she was responding to it or if it was responding to her. "Go ahead then. We have work to do."

She turned to those who had chosen to stay and listen.

Jack called out as he left with his group, "You *want* to die, don't you?"

Michelle barked a laugh at that. "I intend to live forever and, so far, it looks like I'm doing quite well. Make sure you are clear of the forest as quickly as possible. Things are about to change."

"You're crazy!"

Michelle laughed again, "Thank you!" After he left, she leaned into the group huddled behind the protective Ogres and explained her plan.

CHAPTER 4

"Okay," said Arthur in little more than a whisper. "They're gone. We can go now."

Shannon was the first to come out. "What was that?"

"A bunch of Goblins," said Arthur.

"You know what I mean. The *big* thing," said Shannon. "Look at all the trees it pushed out of the way."

Caitlin didn't need Shannon to point. Even this far away, it was easy to see that something large had come through. Trees on either side of the trail were broken or leaning at odd angles. They were too far from the trail to judge how wide it must have been, but Caitlin was pretty sure it was a lot wider than any elephant she had ever seen.

"Remember those weird Dragons we saw back at the house. The ones we got rid of by throwing diapers at them?" said Arthur.

"Yeah," said Shannon.

"Kind of like that but a lot bigger and pointier."

"It is called a Wyrm," said the old man. "But if it is that big, it must be one of the lesser demons. And I suppose 'Dragon' works."

"What's a lesser demon?" asked Shannon.

"It's a long story," said the old man.

"And we have a long walk!" added Caitlin.

"Not as long as you might hope. We are not far from the cave entrance. Once inside we must move quickly and quietly. This will mean no talking until we are away from the main corridor and into one of the secondary veins," said the old man. "We must spend our few remaining minutes discussing how things will go once underground. Then, if there is time, we may discuss lesser demons."

They restarted their hike on the trail winding into the woods with their large Ogre protector in tow.

The old man started up again, "The cave opening will be hidden but large. We must approach carefully. The entrance may be guarded from either the inside or outside or both. We will be most vulnerable just before and just after we enter, for our eyes will not have adjusted."

Caitlin only half-listened as the old man went on and on. She wasn't happy to hear that they wouldn't be able to use their flashlights until they were well into the darkness.

At least Buddy had his stone. He was behind her in their single-file line. Caitlin was still thinking about Buddy turning into an Ogre. She wondered if it hurt him to turn into an Ogre. She could hear his limp behind her, his off-rhythm steps almost sounding like a slow heartbeat. She took the opportunity of a sharp turn in the trail to glance back at him. His eyes were still closed and his face passive.

Without looking up he said, "Don't worry, Caitlin. I'll be okay."

She pursed her lips in the surprise of being caught checking him and whispered back, "I know, Buddy. Does it hurt?"

"No. It doesn't feel like anything," he said.

"But you're limping!" she said.

"Yeah. That's because one leg is longer now," he replied.

Caitlin thought about that. The Ogres were large, quick and strong but poorly proportioned. She saw in her mind's eye Buddy getting bigger and bigger and more and more ill-proportioned until he looked like an Ogre. If it didn't hurt, was it such a bad thing? He would look different, but who cares what you look like?

". . . and if you hear a popping sound like popcorn make sure you immediately . . ." the old man droned on with his instructions.

Caitlin was concerned about Buddy. She wanted to help him get better. She didn't even know if you could get better from what he had. It had something to do with sharing blood with the Ogres back when he had jumped into the garage. If she was going to help, she needed to know more.

". . . different people so you must remember to follow –"

Caitlin interrupted him. "Excuse me."

"What is it?" the old man asked.

"Please tell us more about why Buddy is turning into an Ogre and how we can help him," she said.

The old man stopped and turned to face the three of them, "It is very important that we get to the deeps and find new guardians. Your parents will be hard-pressed to keep the barrier viable. We must spend this valuable time preparing for the challenges of being underground. It will be dangerous and, if we do not prepare, bad things may happen. We can talk of Arthur's affliction later."

Caitlin was unperturbed. "You said our parents couldn't come with us because we would need to go small places to avoid dangerous places. If Buddy becomes an Ogre while we are down there, we will either need to leave him or go into dangerous places we didn't want to go."

"Yeah!" said Shannon, chiming in.

The old man looked at each in turn then threw up his hands, once again continuing the trek. "He has shared blood with an Ogre. This has bound them to him and that is why they help us. However,

44

the binding is not without cost. With Ogre blood in his system, he will slowly become one himself."

"How long will it take?" asked Shannon.

"That depends on him. The speed, strength and size of the Ogres is not natural. Their blood has been contaminated by something dark. They use their emotions – rage, anger, fear – to feed their physical powers, but at a cost. The darkness in their blood feasts on this emotional energy, reinforcing it and creating imbalance. The imbalance is manifested by the body – great size, but poor proportion."

"So . . . I can't get angry?" asked Buddy.

"No. You can get angry and it will not feed your transformation," answered the old man. "It is only when you choose to tap into power fed by that emotion that you will speed your transformation."

"Then why is he limping?" asked Caitlin. "He didn't use anger to do anything yet, did you, Buddy?"

"I did. Remember when Mom was trapped in the trees and the fire was coming?" said Arthur. "Her leg was caught under a tree and I couldn't get it off. I tried to wedge a stick under it but it broke. I got really mad."

"And picked up the tree?" asked Shannon.

"Yeah," said Buddy. "I knew I wouldn't be able to lift it, but I had to try. I couldn't let Mom be burned. Then the tree moved. I still had the stone in my hand. I felt it happen. I felt my body change."

Caitlin asked, "How do we make it stop?"

"All who have been infected have become Ogres," replied the old man.

"It happens to other people?" asked Caitlin, then without waiting for a reply she asked, "The other Ogres, they are Trow aren't they?"

"Yes," said the old man, raising his eyebrows. "The last one to become infected becomes the leader. The group within the chain of infection is then bound to him or her."

"I don't like the sound of that," said Buddy. "So, if someone trades blood with an Ogre I will be bound to that person?"

"No. Only those earlier in the infection chain," answered the old man. "The six Ogres that attacked your house were a single infection chain. You happened to trade blood with the leader, the last one infected. Because of this, you became the leader of the entire chain. Had you traded blood with one of the Ogres in the middle of the infection chain, say the third one infected, you would have bound the first three to you and the remaining three would have remained bound to the last one infected. You were lucky to have traded blood with the leader."

"Lucky me," said Arthur. "You made it sound like they did it on purpose, keeping the infection chain in a single line."

"Yes, they did," answered the old man. "The Trow are ruthless and use any advantage they can find. Once they learned that Ogres were created by a dark infection that could be intentionally propagated and controlled, they began creating

46

groups of infection chains called Death Squads. They are used to commit the most difficult and evil tasks."

"Why did they only send six Ogres? Why not a hundred. Don't they have enough?" asked Shannon.

"Many more than that, but imagine what would have happened if Arthur had become the leader of one-hundred Ogres? It is too dangerous to send that many," answered the old man. "Long ago, in a different age, something akin to that did happen. The Trow do not make the same mistake twice. Most Death Squads are now at least three in number but no more than five. The fact that they sent six is unusual."

"But if it is that easy to bind the Ogres, why haven't they stolen them back?" asked Arthur.

Caitlin watched the old man as he hesitated. "Those who are infected are forced against their will to do so. Most would rather die than to become infected."

"What?" asked Shannon. "Why?"

"Think of it," answered the old man. "You are given great power only to be bound to the next member in the chain. You are forced to do their bidding no matter how heinous, no matter your former will. Even if you are the last in the infection chain, the leader, you will eventually be bound to another, either intentionally when one of your group is lost and the chain needs to be extended, or accidentally, as happened with Arthur. To become an Ogre is a death sentence of free will. None take this sentence willingly."

Caitlin looked back at the Ogre following them along the trail as their protector. Ever since the garage, they had kept her safe. She had begun to consider them friends. Now that she knew that it had no choice in the matter, she wasn't sure how to feel. Does it matter that they had protected her, or should she reserve her friendship to only those who do so under their own free will?

She felt sorry for him. That much was certain.

"I don't get it. Then how do they get any Ogres at all?" asked Shannon.

"It is a simple thing to transfer blood, causing the infection," answered the old man.

"Yea, but if someone infected me, I wouldn't do anything they wanted. I would probably just decide to fight against them! I'd be big and strong enough. You said they were nearly unstoppable," said Shannon.

"You underestimate the Trow," said the old man. "What if they had your family hidden away and under their control? Would you then do their bidding to keep your family safe?"

Shannon didn't answer.

There were very few living things in this world that Caitlin didn't like, but the Trow were definitely on that short list.

"But how do we help Buddy?" asked Caitlin again.

"He must not trade blood with any living thing. This will prevent him from infecting another and becoming bound to them," answered the old man. "And he must not use the strength given to him by the infection. Using it will speed his transformation."

"But how do we stop it?" asked Caitlin.

"You cannot," answered the old man turning to the three of them. "And now the time for questions has ended. We have arrived at the entrance."

CHAPTER 5

"So that's the plan," finished Michelle.

It wasn't the most complicated plan and, because time was of the essence, she had explained it as quickly as possible. As soon as she finished, Bryan blew a low whistle, shaking his head. She saw that Judd's hands went from his hips to the sides of his head. She looked around to see most of the twenty or so people giving her similar reactions.

"I like it!" said Jenn. Judd gave her a look soliciting another comment from Jenn, "No. Really."

"Do you think it will work?" Marci asked.

"It has to," answered Michelle. "But I can't guarantee anything. Peter and I can do a lot with our stones and will do our best to keep everyone from getting hurt, but I can't promise that no one will get hurt."

"It's a good plan. I like it," said Jenn again, smiling broadly. "It's definitely going to work." She then turned to Erin. "Right, Erin?"

Erin made a wide-eyed face at Jenn before sighing and turning to Michelle. "Do we have to send the Ogres away?" asked Erin. "They are basically the only thing keeping us alive."

"Yes," said Michelle.

"Michelle, friends aren't supposed to let friends do stupid things –"

"– alone!" Jenn said, finishing the sentence.

"You stole my line," said Erin, cracking a smile.

"Um . . . ladies?" broke in Judd. "There are a few hundred mean little men with rusty knives that are about a nanosecond from crossing that stream and coming to get us. Can we please decide if we are going with the crazy plan or not?"

"I vote for the crazy plan!" said Jenn, raising her hand and pulling Judd's hand up along as well.

"Me too," said Erin, raising her studded white-gloved hand.

Bryan and Marci looked at each other for a second then they both raised their hands. With that, the rest of the group gave their consent for the crazy plan.

"Good!" said Michelle. "Here goes nothing."

***

Peter thought he'd learned the only limitation of the Ogres when the Goblins surrounded them and tried to blind them as Buddy had done. But now, in their battle to bring down the dam against the Orcs, he saw another limitation exposed and exploited.

When Peter and the Ogre attacked the first dam, there were as many Orcs as Arthur had warned. When Arthur described the Orcs, he imagined a smaller Ogre, but they were nothing alike. The Ogres looked like an ill-proportioned, oversized, hairless gorillas. The orcs had very piggish faces with short upturned noses and large tusks jutting out from their lower jaw. They were large, about a head taller than Peter, and likely outweighed him by at least one-hundred pounds. They had broad shoulders and thick waists, covered with leather armor and haphazard metal plates. As Arthur had warned, they were armed with long, heavy swords and, if first impressions provided any insight, Peter was willing to bet dollars to dimes that they knew how to use them.

As soon as the Ogre saw the dam with five or so Orcs standing in front, it bull-rushed them as befit its size and strength. The two teams of three Peters had run up either side of the streambed and moved to flank those protecting the dam. The Orcs must have been expected such a maneuver because as soon as the teams of three took up position, they were simultaneously ambushed by Orcs from behind. Peter had expected the potential for such a move, and they were ready when it happened, but he had hoped that the defenders wouldn't be so organized.

It was one thing to overcome a team of monstrously strong defenders. It was quite another to learn that they operated as a coordinated unit and understood the tactical nuances that could make the difference in a battle such as this one. However, when one side had a nuclear bomb of a freight train running right at the dam, tactics didn't help much. They didn't need to defeat the Orcs. They needed to demolish the dam and then retreat. And if there is one thing Ogres are good at, it is demolishing things. Peter had seen that first hand when they leveled his house in a few short minutes.

As the Orcs attacked from behind, Peter did some quick math and noted that one Orc was missing from the ten Buddy had seen. He figured that was important, but before he could speculate where the tenth Orc may be, they were on him.

Two Orcs attacked each of the teams on either side of the stream. Their swords were almost as long as Peter was tall, and they worked in pairs, with one making wide arc swings while the other made short quick stabbing motions whenever one of Peter's twins tried to take advantage of the first Orcs backswing. It was an effective way to keep them at bay but did little to threaten them. All they had to do was stay out of reach by yielding ground. Peter became suspicious that the Orcs may be herding them into a trap, so he made note to control the direction of their movements.

Peter didn't need to look to see where the Ogre was. The mud was thicker in the stream and Peter's twins had gotten into position before the Ogre, only a few short steps from impacting the dam. Water had pooled just before the hastily built dam and each step the Ogre took sent sprays of muddy water in every direction. Five of the Orcs were standing in front of the dam with weapons raised, and they called out taunts causing the Ogre to redouble its speed and let out a deafening roar.

Something wasn't right. The Orcs were standing right where the Ogre was going to hit, and they didn't seem concerned. In fact, they were drawing its attention and egging it on. It didn't make sense. And the Orcs that were attacking Peter's twins didn't seem to be too concerned with trying to land blows. It was almost as if they were working to hold their attention. But why?

The side of one of his faces was struck with the knee-high muddy water as the Ogre closed the remaining distance to the dam.

"No!" shouted all of the twins at the same time as they realized what was happening. "Stop! Stop now!"

But it was too late.

The steady beat of the Ogres footfalls was interrupted as he fell into a muddy, water-filled pit a few steps in front of the dam. The momentum of its charge created a wave that crashed harmlessly into the Orcs standing in front of the dam. The hole must have been deep, because the Ogre's entire body disappeared below the surface of the water. According to the old man, only moving water created the magical pressure to hold the creatures back, but when the Ogre didn't reappear after a second or two, Peter began to worry.

Was it trapped under the water? Was it unable to swim or perhaps too heavy to swim? Even though it must have weighed a good half ton, he would've been very surprised if it couldn't swim. He had seen Ogres perform monumental tasks of strength. It should be able to jump off the bottom. Unless the bottom was thick, sticky mud.

Of course it was.

Peter's mind raced with all of these thoughts as he fought off the attacking Orcs assigned to distract his team while the others trapped the Ogre.

The Orcs positioned in front of the dam turned and chopped at the dam with their long heavy swords. Why would they want to open the dam now? If they brought down the dam . . .

Again, Peter's mind caught up with the Orcs plan too late. Bringing down the dam would allow the water to flow and bring up the containment field on top of the trapped Ogre. Peter didn't know what that would do, but he was pretty sure it was bad news for the Ogre.

He was frustrated with himself. They needed to stop reacting and get a step ahead of the Orcs. He needed to think, but there was no time.

What he would do if he were the Orcs? He focused on what they were doing, what they wanted and what they might be thinking.

Somewhere in one of his twins, in one of the six manifestations of himself, he felt the stone come alive, and it hurt.

It wasn't pain or heat. In fact, it wasn't physical at all. It was a pressure within his mind, a thought pressure he felt across his being. He didn't have time to think about where the pressure was coming from or what it was pressing against, because suddenly it burst in release.

Everyone stopped for a half second. All of his twins stopped. All of the Orcs stopped. The water over where the Ogre had fallen was still.

His mind had just exploded. He felt it. But what had it exploded into? Where was the new mental space? What had it been pushing against?

Peter grew still and observed his thoughts. He could feel the heat and humidity of the early afternoon. The sun felt hot on all six of his faces. He could smell the thick, musty pine wood and wet earth odor of the forest. The weight of his weapons felt solid. Some had light rusty knives with too small handles, others had longer Trow swords with wire wound handles, and others still held long and heavy battle swords with thick leather grips. Some of him were wet from the wave created by the Ogre, feet still cool in the pooled water. Peter's mind started with a realization of what he was experiencing.

No longer was his vision split between the twelve eyes of his twins. Now he was seeing through twenty-two. His consciousness had expanded. He was now seeing what the Orcs saw, feeling what they felt. All this he realized in the half-second when everyone paused.

The half-second passed, and the Orcs started attacking once again. This time it was clear that they would not be satisfied with simple distraction. The blows came down heavy, and it was their turn to give up ground.

CHAPTER 6

The sudden change in the Orc's attack, from the somewhat predictably rhythmic slash and recover tactic to a confusing flurry of syncopated strikes, feints and coordinated movement, would have overtaken Peter's two teams of three had he not been expecting it. But he had been.

He learned a lot in the half-second pause when his mind seemed to explode into the space that was the Orcs, and he was trying to figure out how to make use of what he had learned.

He knew the Orcs had set them up from the beginning. They wanted to be attacked. They knew an Ogre would be coming and accounted for it perfectly. They had intentionally kept Peter's twins busy, but not hard-pressed. If they had over-pressed Peter's twins the Ogre might have been called away from the dam to help, away from the trap they had laid for it. He knew that there were more dams behind this one. He didn't know how many, but there would be more.

At first, when he realized he could see out of the Orc's eyes, hear what they heard, feel what they felt, he figured he should be able to read their thoughts. It only made sense. His consciousness was spread over his twins and when his mind expanded into the Orc's he expected it to be the same. But he realized it was not the same. He could feel the mental space of their consciousness and feel the sensations of their bodies, but that was it. He couldn't sense any thoughts or emotions.

He tried to will the Orcs to stop attacking. But either he wasn't doing it correctly or it wasn't possible. He reflected that the stones really should come with an explicit instruction manual rather than a ten-minute cryptic discussion with a crazy old man.

He realized, however, that he didn't need to read their minds to know their thoughts. He had full exposure to their senses. That meant he knew what they were sensing, but more importantly, he knew what held their focus. Just like a mother in a noisy crowd can pick out the sound of her child crying, the Orcs were filtering what attention they gave to their senses, and that told Peter just about everything he needed to know.

He observed how the Orcs by the dam were pulling and hacking at the dam, working to let the water flow. The fact that they were unconcerned about the Ogre trapped below the surface of the water spoke volumes about the confidence they had in their trap. The way they ripped at the dam showed they had no intention to rebuild after raising the magical barrier over the Ogre.

It was all good to know, but he couldn't see how this knowledge helped his situation. Still, his sight kept him alive as the Orcs pressed him with their creative attacks, but he needed more than that just to stay alive. He needed to save the Ogre and then clear the dams, and not just this one.

He centered himself and decided to take one step at a time. First order of business was to save the Ogre and that meant not letting the Orcs tear down the dam.

***

Billy led the group of ten and the Ogre along the side of the dry streambed. He had his finger on his rifle's trigger as they advanced towards the fighting. His impulse was to charge into the battle to help as quickly as possible, but after having been ambushed by the Trow with Judd trying to round up support in the neighborhood, he'd learned his lesson. He wasn't taking anything for granted.

He could hear the scraping of metal on metal and the cacophony of shouting, but what was absent was the Ogre's roar. He was sure he had heard it when they first hit the trail, and the fact that he could no longer hear it didn't sit well with him. If whatever Peter was fighting had taken down one of the Ogres, they had to use caution.

He glanced back at those following him through the clinging, thick brush. Only two or three of them had guns. The rest had what was best described as makeshift weapons harvested from Bryan and Marcie's renaissance fair armory. Some of the recreated weapons looked solid enough, but none were very sharp, and he wouldn't have been surprised if they broke on first impact. They were lucky to have the guns they did, but that didn't ensure victory. Not by a longshot.

That was something else the Trow had taught him. Just because he brought a gun to a sword fight didn't mean he was sure to win. It should have been like when Indiana Jones shot the sword-wielding Arab in *Raiders of the Lost Ark*; one shot and done. But no, the Trow didn't stand still waiting to be shot. They ambushed you and got so close that you didn't have time to shoot them, or they tried to harass you from afar to trick you into wasting bullets or they'd even spur you into chasing them into an ambush.

Billy glanced up into the trees, remembering how he and Judd had chased a routed group of Trow through the neighborhood only to be ambushed from above when they passed under a group of old oak trees. Judd earned some stiches with that one.

Billy was a good shot. No, he was a great shot. But there were more bad guys than bullets in his pocket and he was sure that, by the end of the day, he was going to need every single one of them.

He was the first to gain sight of the battle. What he saw caused him to stop dead in his tracks. "What are they doing?" he asked himself aloud.

One of the ten, John, stepped up beside Billy, "I thought we were supposed to bring down the dam?"

"Yeah, so did I."

"Then what the heck are they doing?" asked John.

"I haven't the foggiest," said Billy, taking off his red Braves cap and wiping his forehead.

The group of ten took in the scene before them to get their bearings. There were at least eight large warthog-humanoid crossbreeds facing off with Peter's six twins. This was not unexpected, however startling it should have been on any other day.

What threw them off was Peter's twins standing between the Orcs and the dam. Every time the Orcs gained an advantage, they used it to hack away at that dam, and this caused Peter's twins to redouble their effort to regain the lost ground and push the Orcs away from the dam. The Orcs seemed to be gaining quite a few advantages. There were little streams of water coming through the dam in places where the Orcs had done significant damage.

"Are you sure they wanted us to bring the dam down?" asked a pike-wielding plumber from Saluda Lane. "It looks like he's trying to keep the dam up, Billy!"

"Um . . ." said Billy. "No, I'm pretty sure we are supposed to bring the dam down."

"Pretty sure or definitely sure?" asked John.

Billy muttered under his breath, "For crying out loud," then yelled over to Peter, "Hey, Peter!"

"Busy!" yelled back one of the twins. "Battling!"

"Yeah! We can see that," yelled Billy. "We want to help, but we aren't sure how. Is the dam coming down or staying up?"

"Long story!" shouted Peter. "Just get the Orcs off me and don't let anyone go in the water!"

That was good enough for Billy. He jogged his crew into a position where they could flank the Orcs without entering the water, but they didn't even have to engage.

Billy dropped to one knee, got one of them in his rifle sight and brought the Orc down. After the second one, the Orcs retreated upstream, leaving Peter's twins and Billy's group alone with the dam.

Getting rid of the Orcs was the easy part. As soon as they left, Peter came rushing over to Billy to explain how the Ogre he had brought with him had fallen into a hole right in front of the dam. And that had been at least a few minutes ago. Billy knew what that meant.

He prayed the Ogre had lungs of a whale, because its chances were slim at best. He called the Ogre he brought with them and they organized a rescue effort.

Billy's first thought was to take a log from the dam and use it to fish out the Ogre from the hole. If it were still alive, it would probably get the idea and grab onto the log. Peter vetoed the idea, saying that if they took a log from the dam it might let water

64

through and activate the barrier. Apparently, this was a bad thing for the trapped Ogre.

Billy's Ogre was listening and didn't wait. Billy ducked at the sound of smashing as it punched through the base of a nearby tree, then watched as the fifty-foot tree came crashing down across the stream.

While fighting the Trow in the neighborhood, he had seen the strength the Ogres possessed, but he realized he had only seen a fraction of the monster's true power when the Ogre lifted the massive tree and dipped it into the muddy water in front of the dam. The tree had to be at least two or three tons.

Billy called out to the group to keep a lookout for potential surprise attacks but kept his eyes on the rescue effort. Suddenly, the tree jerked down twice. Without hesitating, the Ogre yanked hard as if he'd caught a massive fish, and pulled up the log, hand over hand. Almost all of the fifty-foot pine tree was removed when the second Ogre came blasting out, breaking the surface of the water.

The crowd let out of chorus of cheers as the Ogres spat defiant roars into the air.

Billy heard one of the Peter's mutter to himself, "Hard to kill indeed."

"So, we takin' this baby down or what?" Billy asked.

"Yup," said Peter, grinning.

"Bring it down!" shouted Billy.

A second cheer came when the two Ogres ripped the dam apart. Despite taking precaution to stand to the side as the water broke through, both Ogres were thrown back by an invisible gale-force wind as the magic barrier was reactivated. Billy shouldered his weapon and watched the water flowing down the stream. He hadn't walked these trails much; he preferred to be on the lake in his boat. But it looked a good two or three feet higher than he remembered seeing in the spring. He hoped that would be plenty for the barrier.

Peter was still standing next to him. He didn't look none too happy either. "Why the long face?" asked Billy. "We got the dam. The Ogre is fine."

Peter shook his head and looked upstream. "We got this dam. But there are more. We aren't done yet. Look at the water."

Billy looked again. The water was already lower on the banks. He watched for a few seconds and could see the water becoming shallower. He thought about the others. "We need to warn the other group. There was an army of Goblins about to cross when we left them."

Billy grabbed the nearest man and sent him running back to the larger group to relay that there were more dams. Billy turned back to Peter.

"We need to take down the rest of the dams," said Peter in a flat tone.

"Back at the bridge there were a few hundred Goblins about to cross. If we don't go back to help the others, they aren't going to last too long. There are kids there, Peter," said Billy.

"What?" said Peter now giving Billy his full attention. "The kids are there? Why would you bring them here?"

"Things aren't any better in the neighborhood. It is better to keep everyone together," said Billy.

"How many are with them?" asked Peter.

"About twenty. Everyone is armed, even a few guns, but those bullets will run out quickly against a few hundred Goblins," said Billy.

Peter looked upstream and then back to the main trail by the bridges. He noticed Peter's white knuckles as he clenched his fists. For Billy there wasn't much of a decision. "Peter, we have to go back now. What use is the barrier if our families are overrun by the Goblins?"

"You're right. But if we don't take down the dams and get the barrier up more and more Goblins will get through. And they are just the start. We won't be able to run far enough. There won't be anywhere to go."

They both paused for a minute, watching the flow of the stream diminish to nothing. Once again, the bed was stones and mud.

Billy looked back to Peter. "Well. If the choice is dying today or tomorrow, I choose tomorrow. Let's get our families out of here. You coming?"

Peter didn't look at Billy. "I can't."

"Why not?" asked Billy. "We can't beat that many Goblins, but we sure can make a retreat with the Ogres covering us."

"I can't leave. Shannon, Arthur and Caitlin are down there somewhere. If we don't get the barrier up soon, I don't think I will ever see them again. I can't leave."

Billy had forgotten about that. Peter's kids were on the other side of the stream trying to find something in some cave. He didn't really understand all of what was going on but that much he knew. When they got back, they would need to fight their way back to the bridges, but if the barrier wasn't up, getting to the bridges wouldn't be enough. Depending on how long it took them to come back and, judging by the way the Trow had shut down the neighborhood on a few short hours, he wouldn't be surprised if most of the surrounding counties would be overrun when they returned.

"What about Michelle and William?" asked Billy. He felt sorry before he had even finished the sentence. Peter shut his eyes hard and didn't respond. "Sorry," said Billy. "But we have to go, Peter. We'll leave the muddy Ogre with you. It would be a big help if you decided to come along."

When Peter didn't respond, Billy turned to the group and began to shout, "Alright, let's get –"

He was stopped mid-sentence when someone called the alarm. Something was coming at the group through the woods. The

Ogres moved to the front of the group, but then slackened when they saw who it was.

It was a runner from Michelle's group. He found Billy and started talking, and within the first few sentences, Peter had come over listening. After the report had been given, Billy blinked his eyes slowly a few times.

Peter broke the stunned silence first. "I *love* this plan!"

Billy looked at Peter then asked the runner. "Are you sure this is what they want to do? Who told you this? Whose idea is this?"

"That's what they said. It's Michelle's idea," replied the runner, shrugging his shoulders.

"If I could marry this plan I would. Seriously," said Peter with a much cheerier disposition than he had shown a few minutes before. He turned to Billy slapping him on the back. "I hope you're excited, because I am."

"It's a suicide mission," said Billy.

"It's our only chance," said Peter, still smiling, "What more could we ask for than a chance?"

Billy rolled his eyes and sighed then shouted to the group, "Everyone group up! We are going back to the bridges. We have more work to do!"

CHAPTER 7

Michelle was surprised at how quickly Billy's group came back. She, Erin, Bryan, Marci, Judd and Jenn were standing behind the two Ogres who were, in turn, acting as a wall of flesh and bone between them and the Goblins. Fortunately, the Goblins were still hesitating. At least that was what Michelle hoped they were doing. Their scout had said there was something very large coming behind the Goblins. She hoped they were hesitating and not waiting.

Erin was the first to see them coming and she ran over to check on Billy. Michelle walked over with William on her hip, each step sending small but very real stabs of pain up her leg. She saw one of the Peters before she had to think about what she would do if she didn't see him. She and William gave him a big hug.

"William!" said Peter making a fuss over his smallest child. "I'm happy to see you, kiddo." He kissed Williams neck between his shoulder and ear, soliciting giggles.

"Careful," said Michelle. "He has the black stone."

"What?" said Peter. "How did he get that?"

"Long story," replied Michelle as they made their way back to the makeshift battlements. They had to walk away from the bridges to enter since either side of the trail was flanked with walls created by piles of interwoven branches and logs.

"Nice," said Peter as they entered the forest fortress. Two sets of Peters took up positions on either side outside of the fortress. The remaining Peter, other than the one that stood with her, took up position with the Ogres at the front of the trail.

"Hey!" said Jenn to Billy, Peter and the rest of the crew. "Is everyone ready?"

"Do we really need to send the Ogres away?" asked Billy.

"Yup," said Michelle, "If we don't they are going to get hurt."

"It's too dangerous for the Ogres, but we're going to stay?" asked Billy.

"Not all of us."

She went through the plan with Billy's group. It took less than a minute for everyone to say their goodbyes and get arranged, and the group that was leaving positioned themselves in the back of the battlement and the other group took the front. The group in the back had the five Ogres, Billy, Erin, one of the Peters, five other parents and all the children except for William. That left Michelle, five Peters, Judd, Jenn, Marci, Bryan and about fifteen others in the front group.

Now that the Ogres were at the back of the group, the Goblins looked like they were considering attacking. Michelle was pretty sure that when the back group left with the Ogres, the Goblins would pounce. She had accounted for that.

But they needed to keep the Goblins on the other side of the river to keep the barrier from imploding. The best way to do that was to attack them before they crossed. This would force the battle onto the other side of the river. Of course, that meant that twenty-five or so of them would be charging into the midst of a few hundred ill-tempered green Goblins with rusty knives. There was no way they could win that battle, but they didn't need to. They just needed to keep the Goblins on the other side of the river and survive long enough for the second group to do their part.

"Remember," called Michelle back to the second group. "Don't leave until we are all the way on the other side of the bridge. We don't want half the Goblins following you. Wait until we have their full attention."

Billy nodded. Jenn and a few others waved goodbye one last time. Michelle knew what it felt like to leave your kids in a situation like this, but she forced her mind away from the thought and turned to the group.

"Remember. We need to keep the fight on their side of the bridge. Once we start charging we can't stop halfway," she said trying to lock eyes with each person. "We don't have to win. We just need to buy time, so keep in a tight group and watch each other's backs. There are a lot of them but if we stay tight, it should keep them from getting behind anyone."

"Is anyone else excited? I'm excited," asked Jenn.

All six Peters raised their right hands smiling. "Best plan ever."

"I guess," said Bryan.

"What?" asked Marci.

"It will be fun knocking around the Goblins, but . . ."

"But what?" asked Marci.

"Well . . . they're *little*. It is like playing tackle football against a bunch of toddlers. Sure, there's a lot of them but you are sure to win. Where is the fun in that?" he said, looking away.

Michelle heard someone in the back mutter, "You have got to be kidding me."

"Honey, we are going to have –" Marci was interrupted by a deep rumbling sound.

It sounded like a purring crocodile. They all looked up to see a gigantic head winding its way down the trail through the Goblin ranks.

"Is that . . . is that a *Dragon*?" asked Bryan, stumbling backward.

The massive snake-like head wound back and forth on its long sinuous neck as it brought its black clawed feet forward. Its body broadened below the neck where its thick forelegs were attached. It looked to Michelle like an oversized salamander.

"Please tell me that is a Dragon," said Bryan. "Someone please tell me that is a Dragon!"

"I'm not sure," said Marci squinting.

The creature paused a few hundred feet from the bridges and the gurgling rumble rose into a sharp barking sound. Then, lifting its head high, it produced a blast of angry, rolling hell-fire spouting high into the tree canopy. A few of the branches sizzled, turned black and fell to the ground as ash.

"That's a Dragon!" cheered Bryan. "Can you believe this? This is great!"

Peter agreed, offering a high five to Bryan. "Now that's what I'm talking about!"

Marci rolled her eyes and shared a look with Michelle. "Boys."

"Are they serious?" asked Judd.

"It's a *Dungeon and Dragons* thing," answered Michelle over the exalted cheers from Bryan and Peter. To everyone's delight, they only chanted "Dragon! Dragon!" a few times before settling back down.

"Change of plans," said Michelle. "If we all stay in one place, the Dragon –" she paused to let Bryan and Peter share another high five. "– will either bowl us over or douse us with fire. We need a few people to distract the Drag –"

Before she could finish, Bryan and Peter, who were now standing each with an arm around the shoulder of the other, shouted, "Team Dragon!"

Michelle shook her head at them and said, "Okay, okay, fine. You guys get the attention of the Dragon and keep it away from the rest of us. Everyone else, try to keep as many of the Goblins on us and stay tight together. We go on three."

They lined up, with Bryan and the five Peters in the front and the rest behind.

"One . . ." started Michelle.

Either the Goblins sensed something, or they had been waiting for the Dragon, because they charged across the stream and the bridges, growling and roaring in their high-pitched howls, weapons waving in the air.

Michelle shouted, "Three!" and the group of twenty-five raced to meet the charging horde of Goblins and the fire-breathing Dragon.

CHAPTER 8

"How long do we have to wait?" whispered Shannon. "I thought we were in a hurry!"

They had been crouching, hidden behind bushes, watching the cave entrance for what seemed like an eternity. Her thighs were starting to burn from the awkward position they were crouched in, and she was roasting. Her stomach told her that it was after lunch, and during a Georgia summer that meant that it was at least ninety degrees. The old man had assured them that it would be cool, even cold, in the cave, but being dressed in pants and a long shirt was not helping her patience.

"They know what we are trying to do. They would not have left the cave entrance unguarded," said the old man. "We do not want to stumble into any traps."

"I thought the Ogre was supposed to be the decoy," said Shannon. "Let him check it out."

"No!" called Caitlin with a harsh whisper.

"I can see everything," said Arthur with his eyes closed. "I don't see a trap."

Without turning the old man said, "You only see physical reality. There is much more to observe that you cannot possibly see."

Shannon saw Arthur furrow his brows. He beat her to the question. "Everything is made of something. And if it is made of something and is close enough I can see it. There are 560,930 pinecones within a 100-foot radius of our position. There is a snake 526 feet down the trail. There is a family of mice freaking out right now because they can smell the Ogre and, for the first time in their short lives, they are running *toward* a snake. What more is there to observe?"

"Not everything is made of something," replied the old man.

"Name one," said Shannon.

"Time," answered the old man. "Context, shadows, intent, energy, love, malice. Things that can be seen, touched and felt are only a portion of what defines this outside world. Where we are about to go they will mean even less. We will wait a little longer."

"I can see shadows," said Arthur.

The old man shook his head. "What is our inventory?" he asked, changing the subject.

"What?" asked Caitlin.

"What supplies do we still have?"

Shannon started to wiggle her backpack off, but then realized that Arthur was rattling off everything they had, including what was in her bag.

". . . eight granola bars, seven energy bars – two peanut butter and five chocolate chip –, two flashlights between the four of us, one lantern, one homemade spear, night-vision goggles, fifty feet of rope, forty-three ounces of water, a stick of lip gloss, a stuffed kitten . . ."

When Arthur mentioned the stuffed kitten, Caitlin rocked up on her toes and beamed a big smile, leaving little doubt who was holding that particular prize.

When Arthur was complete, they waited while the old man chewed his lip and watched the cave opening. It wasn't the typical bear-type cave Shannon had seen in picture books. Those all seemed to have a nice arched opening that were magically the perfect height for entering so that the explorer would have to duck just a little.

This entrance didn't even look like a cave. It looked more like a large crack in the earth. It reminded her of how the corners of her mouth would crack open in the dry cold winter months. It wandered a good fifty feet from one end to the other and, in most places, it looked like she would have to suck in her breath to fit in. But in the middle it looked wide enough for her Mom's van to drive through and, still, parts of that area had been broken off, probably from when the Dragon came out. The inside was dark. It was impossible to tell how deep it was. She imagined she could solve this whole mess if she could find a large enough needle and strong enough thread. She would simply sew it shut and be done with it.

She was sweating. Shannon didn't think she would be any wetter even if she jumped in a pool. Luckily, it was shaded in the woods, otherwise she was sure the sun on her dark pants and long-sleeved shirt would have roasted her on the spot. She wanted to be in the cool cave air, but she couldn't see a great way to enter. It was just a crack in the earth and there didn't seem to be any gradual sloping entryways, just a sheer drop. Perhaps that was why the old man had approved of the rope.

"Buddy," asked Shannon, "How far into the cave can you see?"

"Pretty far," answered Arthur.

"What do you see?" Shannon asked.

"There is a lot there, but no bad guys," he replied. "You can see the cave entrance. It goes almost straight down forty-five feet and a few inches, then it opens to a larger space. There are six tunnels going off in different directions. Two are really big, like you can drive a truck through. The rest are smaller."

"Do you sense anything alive?" asked the old man.

"Yeah," said Arthur. "There are a lot of living things, "3,349 bats, 15,423 rats, a little more than a quarter-million worms, 238 nests of earwigs . . . Anything else you wanna know?"

"Ugh! Okay, okay, we don't need to hear about every gross thing down there. Are there any bad guys?"

"No. I told you that," said Arthur. "It is just us, the Ogre and basically nature as far as I can see, which is pretty far."

"Well then? Let's go! I'm burning up! We have waited, and nothing is coming. You are the one who rushed us here with your 'Time is short!' rants and so on. Let's go already!"

The old man seemed to hesitate then replied, "Very well. But be on your guard. I am uneasy that the entrance has been left unguarded."

"Yeah. Those Trow are pretty nasty," Shannon agreed.

"The Trow are not our only foe," replied the old man as he got up and started towards the cave. "Take out the rope."

Shannon reached for her backpack but then Buddy said, "It's in the big pocket of Caitlin's backpack."

They stood on the edge of the rocky fissure looking down. Shannon handed the old man the rope. It was smooth and red with a pattern of blue and yellow dots. It looked like climbers rope but was only a little thicker than her thumb. It wasn't thick enough to get a good grip for climbing down.

"It's good we have a rope, but how are we going to get down?" asked Shannon. "I don't think we can climb down this."

"We will be lowered down." The old man waved to the Ogre and the lumbering giant walked over. He tied two loops in one end of the rope. "We will go down two at a time. The first group will be Arthur and me. The second Shannon and Caitlin."

He indicated the two loops he tied in the rope. "Step into these and the Ogre will lower us down."

Arthur stepped forward and put his right foot in the loop. The old man did the same and then nodded to the Ogre, who easily lifted them up by the rope and lowered them down into the cave. The cave floor was shadowed but visible from where Shannon stood. She gave herself the task of peering into the shadows for any danger. She knew Arthur could see everything and would let them know if there was anything dangerous, but it seemed like the thing to do. She noticed that Caitlin seemed to be doing the same thing.

When they reached the bottom, Buddy and the old man silently stepped off and waved. Shannon had expected them to call up, but then reminded herself that they needed to be quiet in the caves. She whispered something to that effect to Caitlin, who nodded in silent agreement. The Ogre pulled up the rope and it was their turn.

Shannon and Caitlin were a little less balanced on the rope than the old man and Arthur had been, but the Ogre lowered them with care and they landed softly on the shadowy, muddy cave floor. The old man waved for them to grab the rope and come over to where they stood, up against one of the walls.

It was cooler already. Not enough to make her comfortable yet, but enough to lend credence to what the old man had said about it being colder down below. And now that they were on the ground, Shannon could see that the cave was really more of a large chamber. It was midday up in the forest and the crack they had used to enter let in a good amount of light, but the cavern was large enough that she couldn't see its far walls. It had a musty basement smell that wasn't altogether unpleasant, and, where the four of them now stood against the wall, she could see two of the six cave entrances that Arthur described.

The old man motioned to them to come in close. They touched heads together, listening to his small whisper. "We will use the smallest of the six entrances. It will be the safest. Once we leave this cavern, all will be dark, and we must keep it so until we are far away from here. Many creatures of the deep will be headed out and this is the only way. For most, their goal will be to escape to the surface, but we must remain unnoticed to ensure we do not become their sport. We will use –"

As if on cue, something large and fast fired out of one of the larger caves on the far side and leapt up through the crack in the ceiling into daylight. It moved too quickly for Shannon to see what it was. Half a second after it left, she felt her hair tickling her cheek as a light breeze brought her some cooler air.

"Hey!" She knocked Buddy on his arm. "Where's our warning?"

"That thing was *fast*. It was gone as soon as it was close enough for me to see," he whispered, shrugging his shoulders. "Besides, it wasn't coming for us. That was obvious."

The old man continued his earlier explanation, unperturbed. "We will use the rope to stay together. We will tie ourselves to each other and move forward slowly until we are in a safer area."

That reminded Shannon of a nature documentary he had seen about climbing mountains. But in that show, it was two mountain climbers who had tied a rope between them and when one fell the other wasn't able to pull him up again. He ended up having to cut the rope. She wondered with dread whether Arthur, Caitlin and the old man would have the strength to pull her up if she fell down a crevasse.

The old man took the rope and tied it around Arthur's waist, then left about six feet of length before tying it around his waist. Then came Caitlin and then Shannon. That made sense to Shannon. She and Arthur were the heaviest of the group, so they needed to be on opposite ends of the rope to act as anchors. If they were too close to each other and they both fell, there wouldn't be enough weight or strength between the old man and Caitlin to stop them all from falling. With Arthur and Shannon on opposite ends, at least they would have a fighting chance.

The old man tucked the extra rope into Shannon's backpack and brought them in close again. "Arthur, can you see the smallest tunnel?"

"Yes."

"That is the one we must take. Once we are in that tunnel, none of us will be able to see. You must guide us down that cave until we reach the next cavern. Stop us once we are there."

"Okay, but that tunnel isn't really —" said Arthur.

"Yes, I know," interrupted the old man.

"What?" asked Caitlin. "What isn't it?

"The tunnel is *really* small. And it isn't round. It's more like a long crack going into the wall. We are going to have to squeeze through," said Arthur.

"Yes, yes, I told you all this. This is why the Ogres and your parents could not accompany us. If we stick to the smaller more difficult tunnels, the chances of us meeting up with something large and toothy is greatly reduced," said the old man. He waved his hand indicating the direction of the tunnel. "We should get going. Stay along the wall."

Arthur led them clockwise along the wall away from the two cave entrances Shannon had been able to see. She ran the fingers of her left hand against the wall, feeling the moist texture of the rock and dirt. Small clumps of loose pebbles and earth fell at her touch. She startled when she felt a furry patch, but then noticed the fine rootlets sprouting from a larger exposed root. She looked up at the crack they had used to enter. It was farther away now, and they were walking away from it. The rope jerked her forward drawing her attention. Caitlin had fallen. Shannon helped the old man pick her up.

"Are you okay?" asked Shannon.

"Yeah," Caitlin whispered back. "I fell in this little hole."

"Not a hole," said Arthur. "It's a claw print."

Shannon squinted at the hole. It was about a foot across and two or three feet deep. There were four of those holes fanned out around a large depression about as wide as she was tall, which she figured was the palm of whatever type of hand or foot made the print.

"Yeah. Smaller tunnels, no bad guys," said Shannon, rolling her eyes.

CHAPTER 9

They continued for what felt like a long time. Shannon realized she must have underestimated the size of the cavern. As they walked, she heard movement from back near the crack in the ceiling. Shannon couldn't help turning to look. She knew Arthur would warn them if something dangerous was coming for them, but it was impossible not to check. From where they were now, the crack in the ceiling almost looked like a waning moon far off in the distance. A few seconds later it disappeared.

"Whoa," Buddy whispered to himself. They all froze.

Then the light came back. She could see the moon-like crack again behind them.

Shannon whispered ahead, "What was that?"

"You don't want to know. It was huge."

"It didn't make any sound," said Caitlin.

"You're right. I think it didn't touch anything somehow," said Arthur.

"Keep moving," said the old man.

They moved at a faster pace even though it was much darker now. Shannon could only see Arthur's outline as he led them along the wall. His steps were much different from the old man's or Caitlin's or even hers. Each step held no hesitation, none of the tentative probing steps the rest took. Once his foot touched the ground there was no adjustment. He was still limping from the changes made to his body by sharing blood with the Ogre, but none of his limp translated into any doubt about how his foot would land.

Shannon found herself wishing she could borrow his stone for a while. Each one of her mostly blind steps held with it a smorgasbord of potential trips and stumbles. It seemed like all the loose rocks in the cavern had ganged up on her and decided to make every step a major pain in the butt.

Arthur stopped the procession. He was facing a wall. "We're here," he whispered.

Shannon looked at the wall. A nice solid wall. "I don't see anything," she said.

"Here," said Arthur taking her hand and pushing it through a crack. It started about waist-high and continued down below the level of the cavern floor where it became a little wider. The crack opening created a space that was like an elevator that had stopped between floors. They would have to squeeze down into it.

"That is *not* a tunnel," said Shannon. "I don't know if I can even fit through there!"

"You can fit. It will be tight, but you will fit," said the old man. "We will have to take off our backpacks and drag them behind us. Make sure that you face –"

"Something is coming our way fast. It's coming right for us," said Buddy in a harsh whisper.

"How fast?" asked the old man.

"Thirty seconds," said Buddy.

They all hesitated.

"Twenty-five."

"Go in!" said the old man too loudly.

"Twenty-two," said Arthur, throwing off his backpack and pushing his way into the crack.

The old man helped push him in. Shannon could hear Arthur's shoes and backpack scraping against the wall.

"Twenty."

The old man wiggled his way into the wall. Caitlin hesitated.

"Eighteen."

"GO!" said Shannon. "You're next!" She looked back to the see the crack-moon shining faintly in the distant dark ceiling. She saw a dark outline coming their way. Bits of dirt thrown up by its charge were visible against the light of the crack.

"Fifteen," called Buddy from within the narrow tunnel.

Caitlin made a whining noise and said, "No, I'm scaaared."

Shannon picked up Caitlin and shoved her into the crack. It had been a bit of a squeeze for Arthur, but Caitlin fit quite easily, even with her backpack on. The old man pulled on his end of the rope while Shannon pushed, forcing Caitlin's body into the crack.

"Twelve."

Shannon could hear it now. Its heavy breathing sounded almost like a horse. She rammed her body into the crack. And didn't fit.

"Nine."

"I don't fit!" shouted Shannon. She tried again, but couldn't get more than halfway in.

"Use your stone!" called the old man.

"I can't," said Shannon. "If I touch you, you'll die!"

"Five!"

Caitlin called from within the tunnel, "Take off your back pack!"

Of course! I'm such an idiot!

She took off her backpack and ducked down to squeeze into the crack, pushing Caitlin forward while holding her backpack behind her. The walls scraped her on either side as she worked herself in. She had to duck as she entered, making the tight fit worse. She could feel her shoulder blades, lower back and knees being cut as she snaked herself deeper.

"One!"

Shannon was sprayed with hot air as the thing pressed its long mouth into the narrow crack and snapped its jaws. Its first lunge missed her shoulder by a hand's width. The thing continued to ram its face into the crack trying to reach her as she forced her way deeper into the tunnel.

Now that she was out of reach and had time to think, she noticed something strange. The creature had remained silent the whole time. There was some noise of course, but no growling or howling.

"Phew, that was close," said Shannon. "I think I see why we wanted the –"

Her body jerked back hard as she was pulled toward the open cavern. Her head cracked against the wall. She didn't understand what was happening. It shouldn't have been able to reach her. Her body was jerked again towards the opening, now pulling Caitlin with her. She screamed.

"What is going on?" asked the old man.

"It has her!" said Arthur. "The rope. It has a hold of the rope and it's pulling us back!"

Crap.

This time she knew what to do.

"Caitlin!" she yelled, struggling as she was pulled further back. "Crawl back in the crack as far as possible. Now!"

She tried to feed as much of the rope back to Caitlin as she could, waited for a count of two, then grabbed the stone in her left pocket.

As always, the abrupt silence greeted her like a bucket of ice water over her head. She shook off the disorientating stillness and untied herself from Caitlin. It wasn't easy; one side was attached to Caitlin and the other was in the mouth of whatever that thing was. It would have been difficult out in open space but wedged in the cavern made it nearly impossible.

The backs of her hands were red with smeared blood by the time she removed herself. She was feeling thirsty too and she knew that, in about a minute or so, she was going to be very hungry. She pushed herself out of the cave, thankful that the beast had been backtracking when she froze time. It had left her a good amount of space to extract herself without risking touching it.

It was dark. About as dark as her bedroom got in the middle of the night without any lights on. Dark enough to step on a Lego on the way to the bathroom, but not so dark that you couldn't find the door.

She couldn't make out the features of the beast, but it was on four legs, looked to be covered with shaggy hair and had a long, toothy snout. She first imagined a wolf, but as her approach gave her a different angle, she realized it didn't fit. Its head wasn't separate from its body the way a wolf's would have been. It was more like a solid torpedo of fur with shortish legs. She wondered if this is what a mole looks like. She had never seen one in real life, so it was possible, but she was pretty sure moles were a lot smaller and had much less in the tooth department.

She changed her angle to get the best use of what little light she had. Her heart leapt and stomach growled when she saw the backpack laying off to the side. She snatched it up and fished out a water bottle and some snacks. As she ate, she rooted through the backpack and found a flashlight. She flicked it on and continued to root. "There!" she exclaimed when she found what she was looking for. She flicked out the Swiss army knife that her dad had put in her backpack and used it to cut the rope a few feet away from the slobbering, foaming mouth of the beast.

Job completed, she sighed, looking back at the tight crack that the old man had laughably called a tunnel. She finished her water bottle and snack then took the rope and backpack with her into the crack. After she had wedged herself a good few feet in, she dropped her stone into her pocket and braced for the silence to be broken.

"Aaaaah!" yelled Caitlin.

"Shannon, you need to cut the rope!" yelled Arthur.

Shannon let them finish before answering. "Settle down. I cut the rope. We have the backpack. We can go now."

"Really?" asked Caitlin.

"Oh," said Arthur to himself. Shannon figured he was just now seeing all that she had done. "Shannon, you're not tied to us anymore."

She mentally kicked herself. She should have done that before she got back in the narrow tunnel. There was no way she was going to get the rope around her waist now and it didn't make sense wasting food to use her stone just to tie the rope around herself in the space of the cavern.

"Yeah, I forgot about that," said Shannon, "I'll tie it around my wrist until we get more room."

"It will be quite a while," said the old man.

"Then let's get going," said Shannon.

As they moved deeper into the tunnel, she heard the beast's heavy footsteps as it moved away from the tunnel. She hoped that it had given up and decided to wander off instead of padding off to another tunnel to head them off further down. The rope tugged at her wrist indicating the others were getting ahead. She pushed the thought from her mind and began shuffling herself down the long narrow tunnel, thinking about what other girls her age were doing right now instead of trying to save the world.

CHAPTER 10

She couldn't see anything, but Caitlin had her eyes open anyway. It wasn't like at night where you could still see a little. She couldn't see *anything*. But it was scarier to move around with her eyes closed, even if she couldn't see anything. Though she did squint a little just in case something sticking out from the wall found her eye.

She may not have been able to see the others, but she knew they were there. She could hear Shannon behind her pushing through narrow spots. Arthur and the old man made less noise but announced their presence with the intermittent tugs on the rope around her waist when their progress outpaced her own. When they first started, Arthur and the old man shot off and essentially dragged Caitlin and Shannon along, but after some quite vocal complaints they found a better matched pace.

She tried to think about how long they had been moving down the tunnel but didn't have much luck. She was pretty sure it had been longer than a *Dora the Explorer*, but perhaps not as long as a Nature documentary. Arthur probably knew. She heard Shannon hit something pretty hard and let out a growl in frustration. The rope around her waist pulled taught from both ends.

"Shannon are you ok?" asked Caitlin.

"No," said Shannon. "I'm terrible. How much longer?"

"I cannot see the end of it. I can only see a few hundred feet," called Arthur.

"How far have we gone?" asked Shannon.

"A little more than a mile," said Arthur.

"This is too much talking," said the old man in a harsh whisper. "Sound does not dissipate the same way down here."

"I don't see anyone that would be listening," said Arthur, "Just the rats, bugs and –"

"Not helping," said Shannon. "I hate bugs."

"Let us rest for a moment. But we must be quiet," said the old man.

Caitlin spent a minute trying to find a way to sit in the narrow confines of the tunnel. She was able to sit with her waist turned so that her shoulders could fit. Her stomach growled.

"I'm hungry," she said. "Is it lunch time yet?"

"I don't know. I don't have a watch," said Buddy.

"Now is a good time to eat and drink," said the old man.

Caitlin pulled her bag around and found a juice box and packet of peanut butter crackers. The crackers were crunched, but they tasted good. It took some patience to get the straw into the right place of the juice box, but she got it. She could hear Shannon and the rest feeling their way to a meal.

"This would be a lot easier with a flashlight," said Shannon.

"No lights," said the old man. "We are still very close to the entrance and the chance for ambush is still there."

"You and your imaginary traps," said Shannon.

"Do you need help Shannon?" asked Caitlin.

"No. I have what I need."

"Shannon?" asked Caitlin. "Why did you say that you couldn't use your stone to get into the crack when the thing was coming?"

"Because you were in the way," replied Shannon.

"So?"

"I can't touch you when I freeze time. It wouldn't be good for you."

"Why?" asked Caitlin.

"Yeah, how do you know?" asked Buddy.

"Because I tried it," said Shannon. "Back in the woods when I was sticking stones in the falling trees so that they wouldn't hit the Ogres. I touched something living."

"What happened?" asked Arthur and Caitlin at the same time.

Caitlin thought she heard the old man exhale heavily. She took another sip from her fruit punch juice box.

"I didn't want to touch anything big in case it came to life and then ran away. If I couldn't catch it again then it might have done a lot of damage while everything was frozen and who knows if it would join real time when I let go of my rock or if it would be stuck in frozen time forever? Or what if touching something living made it die right away? Anyway, I didn't want to touch one of us or a Goblin. I touched trees and stuff and nothing crazy happened, so I figured I should try something more like us."

"What did you touch?" asked Caitlin.

"There was a beetle on the ground near by one of the trees. It was small enough that I figured I could hold on to it if it came to life, but big enough so that I could get a good grip on its leg. I bent down and grabbed it by one of its back legs and then it went crazy."

"How does a bug go crazy?" asked Arthur.

"As soon as I touched it, the beetle became a blur of motion. It was as if it became a mini-tornado right in my hand. It was moving so fast I couldn't see what it was doing. But then, all of the sudden, it stopped moving and became still again in my hand."

Caitlin heard the old man grunt.

"It just stopped moving. I put it back on the ground and let go and it still wasn't moving, so then I started time again and it still didn't move. I think it died," said Shannon. "That is why I couldn't use my stone to get in the tunnel. You were in the way and if I touched you something bad might have happened."

98

"Your sister is correct," said the old man. "Had she touched you while holding her stone, you would not be the same."

"I would have died?" asked a wide-eyed Caitlin.

"That depends," said that old man.

"On what?" asked Shannon. "The beetle died."

"It depends on how long she touched you," said the old man. "Your stone distorts time for whomever touches it. If someone holds the stone and touches someone else, the time distortion is transferred to that person, but in an incomplete way. Because they themselves are not touching the stone, the magic gets distorted."

"So, the magic makes them wiggle around quickly and then die?" asked Arthur.

"No. Shannon, how long did the beetle move in a blur?" asked the old man.

"I don't know," replied Shannon. "Less than ten seconds. Then it stopped moving."

"From your perspective you held the bug for ten seconds. From the bug's perspective, you held it much longer, perhaps a week, maybe two. It wasn't thrashing around in a blur of motion. It was crawling around at its normal pace trying to get away. To you it looked like thrashing because it was experiencing time at a faster rate than you were," said the old man.

"Then why did it die?" asked Arthur.

"It starved to death," said Shannon in a flat tone.

"More likely dehydrated to death, but you get the idea," said the old man. "Each of you have stones of great power. You must take care of how you use them. Your actions carry with them great importance."

"I knew I shouldn't touch anything living, but I thought that if I touched something it would die right out or join frozen time with me," said Shannon. "I'm glad I didn't touch one of the Goblins in the forest. It would have moved too quickly for me to defend myself."

"I'm glad you didn't touch me, Shannon. I was already hungry," said Caitlin. "Old man, why didn't you tell us about that? Why didn't you tell Shannon about her stone?"

"I talked with each of you about your stones," said the old man.

"You didn't tell me that if I touched other people it would speed up their time and kill them, or if I touched an enemy they would be too fast to defend myself. That would have been useful information," said Shannon.

"I told each of you to never touch more than one stone at a time and to never share your stone," said the old man. "That is quite clear to me."

"What happens if I touch someone when I'm holding my stone?" asked Arthur.

"Nothing," said the old man.

"What about mine?" asked Caitlin.

"Yours doesn't do anything," said Shannon.

The hurt of that statement hit her before she could set up defensive mental walls. Caitlin knew her stone was special and that, when she needed it, it would help them, but sometimes she wished she didn't have to wait. Shannon and Arthur both could do super power things, but all hers did was sparkle. She still loved it, but it wasn't easy waiting.

"Sorry," said Shannon.

"It's okay. I like my stone. It will be ready when the time is right, that's all."

"Finish your meals. We must be on our way," said the old man.

"How much longer?" asked Shannon. "I don't fit in here."

"We are about halfway through this particular tunnel. There will be more tight spots but none lasting as long as this one," said the old man.

"You're going to love what's coming next," said Arthur.

CHAPTER 11

Caitlin heard the old man sigh, and then Shannon asked, "What? What's coming next?"

"The tunnel rotates," said Arthur.

"What do you mean *rotates*?" asked Shannon.

"The crack is vertical right now. We can walk or, in your case, slide through. In about fifty yards it starts to rotate counter-clockwise. As far as I can tell, we are going to be sliding on our stomachs soon," said Arthur.

"What?" asked Shannon.

"Well, actually you are going to be on your back. You entered the cave facing the wrong way."

The next hundred yards were filled with Shannon's comments on how she felt about the tunnel. After the tunnel rotated her opinion became quite vehement. It became so grumbly that Caitlin had a hard time making out what Shannon was saying, but the parts she understood made her blush.

"Shannon," called out Arthur. "Kick out your right leg, now."

Caitlin heard a shuffling noise from Shannon and then a small squeak.

"Buddy, what was that?" Shannon asked in a shaky voice. Caitlin strained to hear anything she could in the space between their words. She thought she heard some scratching sounds.

"A rat. It was getting kind of close to your leg," said Buddy. "It's moved away now."

They hadn't gone very far when Arthur called out again, "Shannon, kick again."

More squeaks.

"Buddy, how many?" asked Shannon now with a little more panic in her voice.

"You kicked three." Caitlin could hear something strange in Arthur's voice. "We need to keep moving. Shannon, kick again!"

Even more squeaks. It was getting louder now.

"I can't keep kicking this whole time. I need to keep moving! Give me the . . . ouch! It bit me!" yelled Shannon.

Caitlin froze. She felt Shannon's rope whipped back as she pulled her arms in. She heard Buddy say to himself, "I – I don't know what to do."

"Ouch!" yelled Shannon again.

Caitlin could hear Shannon frantically kicking her arms and legs out. She couldn't see but it must have been a snow angel motion. She didn't have space to do anything else.

Caitlin felt something furry brush by her leg and a mat of gooseflesh ran up her back. She went cold.

"Somebody help me!" yelled Shannon. "Ouch! They are biting me! Help! I can't move! I can't get away!"

She started screaming uncontrollably. Caitlin felt her heart start beating a thousand beats a minute. It wasn't a scream of pain or anger. She had heard those a thousand times before from Shannon. These were screams of terror. Shannon couldn't move as easily as Caitlin could. If they were biting her there wasn't much Shannon could do about it. Caitlin tried to move back to where Shannon was, pulling hard on the rope attaching her to the old man.

"Come on. We have to help!" she called to Arthur and the old man over Shannon's screams.

"Help! Help! Make them stop!" Shannon was yelling. "I can't stop them! I'm stuck! Help!"

Then Caitlin heard the old man shout out, "Ouch! Darn it!"

Buddy called to Caitlin, "There are too many of them! I can see them all. They are all coming right for us. Ouch!"

Caitlin felt a sharp pinch on her leg and let out a yelp of surprise. She rolled her body and swatted at where the pain was and felt something furry go flying away. In the second it took her to realize that she had been bitten, three more sharp pains blossomed on her back.

"Buddy! Use your stone! Help Shannon!" said Caitlin.

"I am using my stone! Ouch! There are too many of them. I can't do anything!" yelled Arthur.

They were all being attacked! What had first felt like a single raindrop of pain was now turning into a steady shower of agony all over Caitlin's body.

"They are biting me everywhere!" yelled Shannon between screams. "Someone help! My face! They are biting my face! I can't stop it!"

Caitlin called out through the torrent of bites. "Shannon use your stone!"

"No! I can't. They will be too fast! I'll die! Help me, please!" yelled Shannon. "They are eating me alive! It hurts too much!"

Caitlin tried to ignore the pain of the rat bites and pulled hard on the rope holding her attached to the old man. She needed to get to Shannon. They were all being bitten, but at least Arthur and the old man could curl up or protect themselves a bit. Shannon was the biggest and the tunnel was too narrow for her to curl up. The best she would be able to do was wave her arms and legs.

The rope didn't budge. She couldn't get any closer.

"Help! Please! Help!" called Shannon.

The intensity of Shannon's screams was fading. And that wasn't because the rats were biting her less.

"Shannon!" called Caitlin, almost on the verge of tears. "Don't stop fighting! Don't stop!"

Arthur and the old man were screaming in pain as well. Caitlin had lost count of how many times she had been bitten. They were all stuck in the narrow, ink-black tunnel with nowhere to go. They were being eaten alive and there was nothing they could do about it.

She needed to do something. She pulled out her stone from her pocket and curled around it to keep it safe from the rats. She could feel them darting in and out, biting all around her wherever they could – on her ear, her legs and the small of her back. She focused on her stone. She ignored the pain of what was around her and focused on her stone.

Caitlin realized what her stone was for. She realized what the old man had been trying to tell her in the basement. She knew what she had to do.

CHAPTER 12

Arthur ran over and jumped on the couch next to her. "It's your turn! He wants to tell you about your stone."

"I haven't used a stone," she said. "He can't tell me secrets about my stone if I haven't used one."

"He said you will use one and that he has to tell you about it before you do," Arthur said, yawning.

She got up and made her way down into the basement. She double-checked to make sure that all the lights were on before going down the stairs. She found him sitting at the small wooden table in the tiled kitchen area, but he didn't look up when she came down. She walked over to the table and sat across from him, then put her hands on the table and looked over at him.

He was sitting with his legs crossed on the wooden chair with his back to the sink. There was a large mirror above the sink, which gave her a view of his back. She could see that his long, grey hair was matted and stuck in places to his brown shirt. Although she was pretty sure it shouldn't be called a shirt. Perhaps a robe? It didn't look like anything she would choose to wear anyway.

She could feel the sand residuals on the table of the poly sand they had gotten for Christmas. Mom made them play with it the basement because of the mess it made. Caitlin didn't mind coming down to the basement during the day to play with the sand or jump in the trampoline as long as someone else was with her. She didn't like being down here at night though. It was kind of scary.

"I don't have a stone, you know," said Caitlin.

"You will," said the old man.

"How do you know?" she asked.

"I have seen it," said the old man.

"You can't. If I haven't done it, you can't see it, unless you can see into the future. Can you do that?" she asked.

"Not quite," said the old man. "Tell me, how old are you right now?"

"I'm turning five soon," said Caitlin, puffing out her chest and sitting up a little straighter.

"Hmmmm ..." said the old man, sounding impressed. "The stone you will carry is perhaps both the most dangerous and wondrous of them all."

"What will it do?" asked Caitlin. "Buddy can do lots of cool stuff with his, like flips and stuff and Shannon can freeze time. What will I be able to do with mine?"

"That is entirely up to you," said the old man.

"What is up to me?" asked Caitlin, tilting her head, the ends of her hair brushing the tabletop.

"You will decide what your stone will do for you," answered the old man. "It will grant you one dream."

"It will grant a wish? Like a genie?" she asked, bouncing in her seat.

"No. Not a wish, a dream," said the old man. "It is not a genie's lamp. You cannot simply ask for a pile of gold and receive it. You must ask for a dream and if you truly want it with all of your being, you will receive it."

"What if I don't?" asked Caitlin.

"Then the stone will not respond," said the old man.

"Okay. I know what I want," said Caitlin, crossing her arms across her chest. "I want all the bad guys coming from the cave to go away."

The old man smiled at her from across the table. "The stone can only be used to create, not to shift reality or change the past."

"What does that mean?" asked Caitlin.

"It can be used to create your dream. It cannot be used to change the way gravity works so that everyone can fly. It cannot be used to change the past either. The stone will not be able to change the fact that the deeps have been opened to this world."

"But I can make things?" asked Caitlin.

"Perhaps."

Caitlin brought her knees up to her chest and wrapped her arms around them as she considered what she might make. "I can't change gravity to make me float, but can I give myself wings to fly with?"

"Yes, I suppose, if that is your dream," said the old man. "Remember, the stone will not respond unless it is a true dream that you want more than anything else. Otherwise the stone will break and become useless forever."

Caitlin considered what he said, worried. "How will I know if my dream is good enough? If I really want it? I don't want to break my stone."

"You must look inside yourself and decide," said the old man. "But be warned that dreams are not simple things. You must protect and feed them lest they wither away and die. A dream is often the smallest spark of life. If you protect it within your soul and fuel it with hope, it will ignite a fire within you that the oceans could not drown. However, just as easily that spark could extinguish from neglect. You must protect your dreams."

"But I don't want to catch fire," said Caitlin.

The old man stared at her. Caitlin tried her best but couldn't help smiling and letting a small giggle escape.

"Very funny," said the old man with a wisp of a smile on his lips.

"I will protect my dream once I figure out what it is," said Caitlin. "Don't worry about that! So I just need to have a dream and then the stone will give it to me. That seems pretty easy."

"A final warning," said the old man, holding a finger up. "To achieve your dream, you must take full responsibility for what you desire. Quite often those closest to you will not see the value of your dream and will try to dissuade you. It was not given to them – it is not for them, so they cannot possibly see the dream for what it is. Do not let others quench the spark of your dream."

"Okaaay . . ." said Caitlin. She thought she understood what he was saying but she couldn't imagine anyone not liking her dream. Of course, she wasn't sure what it would be, but since she would only get one thing from her stone, she figured it was okay to spend some time thinking hard about it. She was pretty sure that once she knew what it was, everyone would like it. How could they not?

She figured that the old man probably didn't have much fun growing up in the deeps. Hadn't he said that he was taken from his family when he was young? She wondered if he remembered his family at all.

Occasionally, Daddy would go on trips away from home, but that wasn't bad. He always came back. It was worse when Mommy left. One time they both left for a whole weekend. Grandma R, the one with parrots, had come to stay with them that time. She really missed Mommy then. She couldn't imagine never seeing her parents again.

She reconsidered the old man. He was sitting there waiting for her next response. His tangled light hair was streaked with grey. His hands were laid out on the table, palms down. His fingernails were bitten down as far as they could go, but by some trick of magic still managed to hold dirt underneath. Even with palms down she could see that he had thick calluses. The tops were dark and held scattered cuts and bruises. She glanced down at her right hand with neat fingernails freshly cut and painted pink by her mother.

"You are trying to take care of us," she said.

"I am trying to help . . ." The old man stopped mid-sentence when Caitlin leapt over the table and wrapped her arms fiercely around him, hugging him for all she was worth.

"Ack!" yelled the old man, trying to wiggle free.

"It's okay, it's okay," Caitlin said over and over. "I'm going to take care of you too."

"Aaargh! Get off!"

The old man squirmed like a pro, but Caitlin was used to holding onto kittens, and even William, when they protested her constrictor-like appreciation. He might as well have been wrestling with a vice for all the good it was doing him.

Eventually, Daddy came down and ended their embrace. Caitlin was beaming when she saw her dad.

"My stone is going to be better than yours," she said.

"I'm sure it will be," said Peter. "Everyone's is."

He picked her up and carried her over to the stairs to get ready for bed.

CHAPTER 13

Caitlin felt the cool wet floor of the narrow tunnel against her cheek. The small particles of dirt and rock stuck against the side of her face. She was curled up around her stone. In the fetal position, she held it close to her stomach with both hands protecting it against the rats.

Her eyes were shut tight as she focused on her stone and her dream. No one was screaming anymore. She couldn't feel the rat bites anymore either. She was so focused on her dream that she wasn't sure if it was because she didn't feel them biting anymore, or they had actually stopped. It didn't matter. She was focused on her dream.

The stone felt warm as she squeezed it in her little hands. Even though her eyes were squeezed shut, light started to shine through her eyelids. At first, it was so dim she figured it was the sparkles that she always saw when she rubbed her eyes a little too hard, but then the light grew brighter and shifted in color. Blasts of color pin-wheeled through her eyelids. First red then yellow and then green and then the rest of the colors, some she didn't even know. It grew in intensity as the colors rotated faster and faster. A deep, low humming noise shook the ground as the rotating colors melded into a single blinding white-hot nexus of light and sound. Somewhere in the background she could hear Buddy yelling something. She couldn't hear what he was saying.

Caitlin shut her eyes tighter against the blinding light but nothing she did seemed to shield her from it. Then suddenly it all stopped.

Being released from the assault of light and sound felt like a physical weight being removed. She felt lighter somehow. However, there was a faint, glowing shimmer of light remaining. She opened her eyes to see if it was her stone. The stone was still in her hand in one piece, but it was not the source of light. She smiled when she saw what it was.

"Hi there," she said.

"Caitlin," asked Buddy, his voice strained. "What is that?"

She giggled as the soft colorful furball of her dream rubbed up against her face, tickling her nose with its hair. Its soft-white glow threw long shadows as it padded around her, rubbing up against her head and back. Caitlin giggled at the attention.

"It's a rainbow kitty!" Caitlin yelled.

"You used your stone to make a rainbow kitty?" asked Arthur.

"Yup!" said Caitlin. "It was my dream."

"Well the rats ran away because of the light, but they're coming back now. You wasted your stone, Caitlin. We need to do something now!" yelled Arthur in a panic.

"Buddy –"

"Too late!" said Arthur. He was frightened. They all were. "Here they come!"

Caitlin didn't need Arthur's warning. She could hear the scampering of thousands of tiny-clawed feet coming at them from everywhere. The acoustics of the cave seemed to distort the noise and it would have sounded like rain if the pitch weren't so high. Caitlin heard Shannon let out a wracking sob of anticipation. It sounded like she had fared far worse than everyone.

"Rainbow kitty?" said Caitlin.

The multicolored feline came to attention at her call, pausing in mid-step with its tail held high, and let out a small meow mixed with the texture of a purr.

"Attack!"

***

Shannon's world was pain.

They had stopped biting when the burst of light scared them off. That left her with the throbbing echo of hurt left by a thousand bites. She could feel small matchhead-sized flaps of skin hanging from her arms and legs where the rats had failed to bite clean through. The first bite had been near her ankle where skin had been available between her pant leg and socks. It had felt like a bee sting or like someone pinching her hard with their nails.

But then they came at full force. Now she knew that the first bite had been tentative, probing, for each time they bit they seemed to bear down harder and hold on for longer. If she didn't pull them off or kick them away, they pulled on her like a dog wrestling for a toy.

She did her best to bat them away with her arms and kick at them with her legs, but there were too many of them and she couldn't move well in the tight space. They crawled all around her and bit wherever they could find an opening, but then they started biting through her cloths. It wasn't long before she was being bitten everywhere, the skin being pulled from her body. It was like being skinned alive.

When they got to her face, she stopped waving her arms and just focused on using her hands to cover her face and eyes. She stopped kicking her legs too, less from a conscious decision and more from the involuntary reflex to curl up into a fetal position. Only she couldn't curl up into a ball. She barely fit in the tunnel as it was. Her knees and head slammed up against the ceiling repeatedly as her body took over and tried to protect itself, writhing like a worm.

Then the light came, and the biting stopped. She wondered if she was dying. She had heard stories about a light at the end of a tunnel, but she could still feel the hard, cold stone tunnel under her body, the unyielding pressure of the ceiling on her stomach causing her to take shallow breaths. She hadn't removed her hands from her face. She wouldn't. Then she heard a low humming noise. It seemed to be coming from everywhere.

Then it all stopped. The light and noise went away.

She could hear Arthur and Caitlin talking, but the throbbing in her head was too loud. She did, however, hear when Arthur said that the rats were coming back. She wanted to scream in rage, but all that came out was a whimper. The pain made her more tired than she had ever been in her life. She knew that if she gave into the urge to relax and fall asleep, she probably wouldn't wake up again. But what could she do? They were coming back and all she could do was try to stay alive for a little while longer.

Red light flashed by her shoulder accompanied by a gust of wind. Chattering squeals erupted all around her. Then blue light swam by other side, and there were more high-pitched screeches and more colors – green, orange, yellow, violet – that pushed back the darkness. The colors flashed all around the cave like a pinwheel firework with her in the center. Thousands and thousands of pain-filled squeals created a discordant echoing chorus.

Then, finally, silence.

She lay, face covered by hands, listening. There was nothing, only her throbbing heartbeat. Then she heard the old man.

"Are they gone?"

"No," said Buddy. "Not gone. Dead. *All* of them are dead."

Shannon felt a wave a relief wash over her. No more bites. It was done. She felt herself crying, unsure if it was from relief or the pain she still felt.

"Go help Shannon," she heard Caitlin say.

She jumped when something soft brushed up against her side. It wasn't a rat though. It was softer and bigger. She pulled her hands away from her face and saw a soft glow moving down around her feet. She couldn't quite see what it was.

"What is it?" asked Shannon in a weak voice.

"It's my dream. I used my stone," answered Caitlin in a gentle voice. "It's my rainbow kitty."

Shannon turned her head around to watch the glowing kitten walk up the left side of her body. It was tiny, perhaps only as tall as one of her hands. Its longhaired fur luminesced with colors that moved across its body like slow motion waves coming to shore. The colored movement reminded Shannon of the lava lamp she had bought at the science museum gift shop.

As it padded closer on soft little feet, it rubbed up against her arm, asking for a pet, which Shannon gave reflexively. She touched the top of her hand on the hard, rocky ceiling of the tunnel and winced in pain. She could see in the kitten's light that the back of her hands were slick with blood and chewed to the bone in places. She tried to hold back the tears at the sight, but it was too much.

The kitten registered her discomfort and turned with a gurgling purr to lick her hand. Shannon would have pulled her hand away had the motion not been so quick. She bore down waiting for the spike of pain, but none came. Instead, her hand started to tingle like it had fallen asleep at the touch of the sandpapery tongue. She brought her hand around closer to her face to look at it, but the kitten doggedly followed the motion continuing to lick the back of her hand. A small giggle escaped at the sight of the purring kitten chasing her hand with its tongue.

Shannon called to the others. "She's licking my hand."

Caitlin giggled her reply. "She's taking care of you, Shannon."

"Wow . . . Shannon, look at your hand!" said Buddy, unable to contain his excitement.

The kitten had finished with her left hand and was now licking her right hand. She brought her left hand up and yelped in surprise.

"What is it?" asked the old man.

"My hand," said Shannon, voice thick with wonder. "There isn't a mark on it. It's completely healed!"

CHAPTER 14

Billy and Erin led the group away from the bridge. They had two of the five Ogres with them in the front. The other three were in back with one of the six Peters. The twenty or so children were in the middle being corralled by five more adults whom Billy had just met. He would have felt bad for not knowing their names if he had time to think about such things. They had just left Jenn, Judd and the rest who were tasked with fighting off a horde of Goblins. Or rather, the job was to keep the horde busy while he and Erin worked on their part of Michelle's plan. Michelle and the rest had to be outnumbered by at least thirty to one.

Billy saw that Erin kept glancing back, probably making sure that all of Jenn's kids were accounted for along with their own. Three of the five adults had arms full of smaller children. The other two, the largest two, were laden with weapons. They had no illusions about safety. The Trow were still roving the area and she wouldn't be surprised if more centipedes ambushed them.

They were scanning all around as they marched single file back along the hard-packed dirt-bike trail. They were coming up on the burning mountain of trees, and they were going to have to leave the trail to get around. Dark black smoke rolled from the still raging fire. The rain they had gotten last night was the only thing keeping the fire from spreading to the rest of the woods. He wasn't sure if that was a good thing or a bad thing. At least a good forest fire might have pushed the Goblins back for a while.

Billy caught Erin's arm when she stumbled over a protruding root in the trail. She sucked in air through her teeth at the stinging pain.

"Sorry," said Billy. "Reflex."

"No. Not your fault," she said. "Thanks."

She gave him a smile that looked forced. The long white gloves hid the damage that had been done to her hands and arms when she fought the centipedes in Jenn's garage. Erin had told him about how she had used bleach and an exploded can of Raid to stop the bugs, but it did a number on her forearms as well. Jenn had slathered her arms up to the elbow with Neosporin then had insisted on the gloves. He didn't envy her for having to wear the gloves in the ninety-degree heat.

They took a wide arc around the burning piles and made it out of the woods without much issue other than more of the children asking to be carried. Erin and Billy's house was right on the lake. They walked along the woodchip path on the manmade earthen dam used to create the lake, then, instead of continuing along the path up to the road where random Trow ambush was likely, they skirted along the lake edge through a few neighbor's yards right into their own back yard.

Walking into the cool air-conditioned house felt like walking into a refrigerator. All the children and most of the parents made loud "Oh!" noises at the cooler environment. Billy watched Erin's face contort as everyone walked in without taking off their shoes. They should have never installed those white carpets.

After hydrating in the air conditioning and chowing down some food, everyone felt much better. The house became too loud for comfort. Billy, Erin and Peter found respite in the backyard near the edge of the lake. The faint sounds of screams and metal clashing mixed oddly with the squeals of children playing in the house. Billy glanced over and saw a column of fire shooting a few-hundred feet into the air somewhere in the forest.

"How many do you think we need?" asked Peter after a long drink of Gatorade.

"No clue. I thought you were a chemist or scientist or something?" said Billy.

"Chemist, yea - but not a demolition expert. I don't know. Let's get at least ten full ones," said Peter.

"I'll get a chain from the garage. I don't think the big guy will be able to carry ten without dropping them," said Erin.

Billy and Peter watched her go around the house up to the garage. Billy looked at Peter out of the side of his vision. He had seen what the stones could do when William grabbed the black one and took out some oversized centipedes, and when Michelle took out a crew of Trow in her backyard with her stone, but Peter's stone was just creepy. There were six of him. They all looked identical. And now that he thought about it, even after each battle they still looked identical. Sure, some of them had dirt marks on their cloths in different places and some had different weapons, but *they* looked identical. He stole a glance at Peter. As he expected, there was a scratch starting at his temple ending near his chin. He had seen that mark before. In fact, he had seen it on each of the other five Peter's. It freaked him out almost as much as his blood red eyes.

"What?" asked Peter turning to look at him.

Crap. "Um . . ." Billy scrambled to find something to say. "I wonder how the other group is doing. I saw flames shoot up a second ago and I think it came from where they are."

"Dragon," Peter replied.

"What?"

"A Dragon came just after we left. They had to split up into two groups, one to keep the Dragon busy and the other to keep the Goblins interested. It's a pretty scrappy tussle, but we shouldn't delay. They won't win, only stall," Peter commented.

"How do you know that?" Billy asked before he realized that he might not want to know the answer.

"I can see it. The rest of me are there. I can see what they see," said Peter.

As he answered, Billy saw him flinch, bringing up a hand to his other cheek. He pulled his hand away from his face to show bright red blood. A new cut had appeared on his face out of nowhere. Blood began running down his face and pooling on the edge of his chin before releasing thick droplets. He sighed and pulled the collar of his shirt against the wound.

"I can feel it too," added Peter.

"Got it!" yelled Erin on her way back. "We had two."

Erin was dragging a heavy chain with two propane tanks looped through. She handed the chain to the Ogre.

"Eight more to go," said Billy, waving them on with his rifle as he walked off into the neighborhood.

The Ogre held the chain up with one hand as it considered the dangling the gas tanks. It looked like a large charm bracelet. Erin's phone gave a buzz. It was a text from Jenn.

"Your phone is working?" asked Peter surprised.

"Yeah."

"Can I use it? I know a guy who should have a lot of propane."

Five minutes later, Brad pulled up in with an SUV full of propane tanks and a few more people. His tires squeaked as he stopped short in the driveway. Apparently, the Ogres gave him pause. Billy and Erin watched from the front door as Peter coaxed Brad and his family out of the safety of their car.

"Who is this guy again?" asked Billy.

"No clue. Peter knows him somehow," said Erin.

Brad and his wife extracted the kids from their car seats while Peter and one of the Ogres unloaded the propane tanks in the back.

"Ugh. They brought kids. We don't need more kids here."

"It's safer here. We have the Ogres."

Billy didn't comment as the little girl with blond curls bounced over to them. Her brother sauntered over with the unlikely combination of confidence and unsteadiness only found in toddlers and drunks. Brad's wife introduced herself.

"Hi, I'm Catherine. Thanks for inviting us over. Things were getting weird over by us. I like your white gloves!" she said to Erin.

"Hi, I'm Erin and this is Billy. Who are these little ones?" asked Erin, kneeling down to tickle the little boy's belly.

Billy was not in the mood for introductions. It had been a long day.

"Nice boat!" Catherine commented.

"What?" asked Billy, thrown off guard by the change in subject.

"Is that 300 horsepower on a fiberglass boat? That thing must fly," said Catherine in an appreciative voice.

"Well, yeah. We had to take it out of the garage to make space for the command room."

"I used to wakeboard. Do you guys waterski?" she asked.

Thankfully, Erin picked up the conversation. He nodded to Catherine and then walked over to where Peter and Brad were collecting the tanks.

"How many?" he asked.

"With these and the two you found we have eight total," said Peter.

"Seems full," said Billy shaking one of the tanks. "That makes our life a lot easier. Thanks for bringing them over."

"I think you mean 'Tanks'," said Brad with a smile.

Billy gave Brad a flat look and chewed on the side of his cheek. He was not in the mood for a smile like that.

"Okay, We need two or three more," said Peter.

"Hey, guys?" asked Catherine who had walked over. "What is the deal with all the propane tanks?"

Peter started to talk, but Billy interrupted him. "Not outside."

Peter nodded, and they shuffled into the house. People, young and old, moved around the house like ants on a hoagie. They sat at the kitchen table that gave them a nice view of the chaotic living room as well as the relative tranquility of the lake. It was noisy, so they needed to raise their voices.

"There is a battle over in the woods that isn't winnable. We need to help contain the bad guys that keep coming out of the cave."

"And how do propane tanks help with that?"

"It was Michelle's idea. The nasties cannot cross moving water. It's something about being creatures of the earth. Anyway, there is a stream that runs around the cave and can keep them all contained if we can get it flowing again," said Peter.

"They made a dam?" asked Brad.

"Yup. We tried to knock the dam down, but they made at least three and they are each heavily guarded. There was no way for us to get them all," said Peter.

"So you are going to blow up the dams with the tanks?" asked Catherine.

"No. It would be hard to get close enough and who knows how many dams they have built," Peter added with a wicked smile sweeping a hand towards the lake, "Think bigger."

Brad paused and then understood, "You cannot be serious."

"If it is moving water they need, then moving water we shall provide," said Peter sweeping his hand to indicate the lake. "They'll never even see it coming."

CHAPTER 17

After Michelle shouted, "Three!" Bryan was the quickest to engage the charging Goblins. He was three or four steps ahead of everyone one else as they charged across the bridge and muddy streambed. If time had been available to reflect, she would have concluded that he had charged before she had even given the signal. There was an audible groan of disapproval from Marci's direction when it became evident that Bryan would be meeting the horde half-a-second before the rest of their group.

The plan had been to keep everyone together in a tight knot so that no one person could be singled out and surrounded by the overwhelming numbers. If they stayed shoulder to shoulder in a tight circle, they could do this.

Michelle had gotten the idea from a children's book Peter's mother had bought for the kids about gladiators. As the book told it, the 'testudo', or tortoise formation was an effective tactic Romans used in the time of Marc Antony. And it would have worked too if the Dragon hadn't showed up.

Unfortunately, standing in 'testudo' would create a perfect target for a fire-breathing Dragon. But if they split up, the horde of Goblins would surround them one by one. Their only chance was to distract the Dragon away from the main group. Otherwise, they wouldn't last more than a few minutes.

That was probably why Bryan had taken off so quickly. He and the five Peters had volunteered, with the enthusiasm typically reserved for school-age children asked to clean out a cake-batter bowl, as the group's official Dragon distractors.

Most of the Goblins had chosen to funnel onto the bridge, not trusting the muddy streambed that had so recently been flushed with water, though a few had started to work their way across the muddy rocks. All five Peters had foregone the bridge and chosen instead the riverbed route.

With his two scimitars waving, Bryan leapt into the air landing on the left-hand side bridge railing. In the same motion, he slashed down low with his scimitar, causing most of the surprised Goblins on the bridge to either duck or, for the unlucky few, lose their heads. Michelle watched in wonder as he took three light steps on the railing and then leapt into the flank of the main body of Goblins trying to force their way onto the bridge. A half-second later the five Peters engaged at the same point, and the diversion was in place. Perhaps all those hours in Bryan's basement playing *Dungeons and Dragons* wasn't a waste of time, after all.

The Goblins on the bridge had lost the momentum and cohesiveness of their charge, for when Bryan and the Peters crashed into the flank of the main body of Goblins, they quelled any potential for the larger group to add the needed momentum to trample their way across the bridge. Michelle forced her focus away from where Bryan and the Peters were fighting and reapplied it to their charge. Her right hand held the Trow sword someone had given her, and in her left she squeezed her stone.

"I am quick. I am fast," she chanted as she ran up the short incline of the bridge, the stone burning her hand in response. "I am lightning quick!"

She took a skip-step to adjust her footing, avoiding the still falling Goblin that Bryan had decapitated a half-second before, then unleashed a fury of blows on the remaining half-distracted Goblins on the bridge.

"I am speed. I am grace," she yelled, ducking under and stepping through what counterattacks the Goblins could muster.

She was too fast. None of them could touch her. Her sword made whipping sounds as it broke through the air as if it were a light stick and she were swatting at flies. She had made it to the other side of the bridge, and, for a brief second, she and the Goblins before her stood still. A quick glance behind her showed

Marci, Jenn, Judd and the others charging across the bridge, awash in Goblin blood provided by her speedy dance. She had cleared the bridge in a second or two, but now that she was on the other side, she needed to be careful. It wouldn't matter how fast she was if she became surrounded. Her stone wasn't going to give her eyes in the back of her head. She reminded herself that they were supposed to stay together.

She heard the Dragon purr its deep, alligator growl and saw it charging down from the trail towards the bridge. The sound seemed to awaken the Goblins who attacked Michelle with reclaimed bravery. Michelle countered the charge with a wide low swipe of her sword.

"Careful now," said a voice right next to her. It was Marci. On her other side was Jenn and she could hear Judd breathing heavily behind her. They were a group now.

"Stay tight to each other and don't let anyone get pulled from the group!" yelled Michelle as the Goblins pressed in once again.

With Marci and Jenn on either side of her, Michelle had to change from wide slashes with her sword to quick parries and jabs. She didn't have the room to swing quite as widely. The Goblins pressed in from all sides, testing their formation. Michelle continued chanting to herself as she ducked, parried and countered. Out of the corner of her eye, she saw Marci fighting from a low crouch. She had a small hatchet in each hand and rather than using them to hack away like an ambidextrous woodcutter, she kept them spinning in her hands as they darted to and fro, blocking attacks and scoring hits. It reminded Michelle of a baton twirler in a marching band, and then she remembered that Marci *was* a baton twirler in college.

Michelle's stone-enhanced speed allowed her to score critical hits with nearly every thrust of her Trow-made sword. Marci, however, took a different tactic. Michelle heard Marci exchange four or five strikes each second. The phrase *death by a thousand cuts* came to Michelle's mind.

"I am fast. I am too quick to see!" she continued chanting to herself as Goblins fell in her wake.

"The Dragon is getting closer," sang Jenn as she used the two-handed battle-axe from Bryan and Marci's basement armory to harvest two Goblin heads in one swing.

Michelle flinched and brought her sword up in a defensive position to block the follow-through of Jenn's mighty swing, but Jenn was able to stop the heavy axe's momentum just before it contacted Michelle's sword.

Jenn noted the move and winked at Michelle. "Don't worry! I'm not going to hit you," then swung the axe in the reverse direction soliciting a yelp of surprise from her other neighbor.

The Dragon snaked its way down the trail to meet them. She had been hoping that it would be slowed by the mass of Goblins at its feet, but, unfortunately, it didn't seem too concerned with their wellbeing as it plowed through the Goblin horde like an out of control eighteen-wheeler through a cornfield.

The Goblins that didn't get out of the way were trampled under its massive claws or thrown to one side. On the bright side, the Dragon was removing more Goblins from the fight, but that also meant it would reach their group in a few short seconds and trample them just the same. And that was if it didn't decide to pull up short and roast them.

Where are Bryan and the Peters?

CHAPTER 18

"The Dragon is moving!" yelled the Peter closest to Bryan.

They had fought their way into the Goblin horde's flank and had become surrounded. Bryan's surprise move of jumping from the bridge into the Goblin flank had bought them an early advantage, and they hacked their way about half the distance to the Dragon. But now they were surrounded by Goblins and the tactical benefit of surprise had evaporated. The six of them had formed a loose circle and pressed their way through the sea of Goblins, but progress had become slow and the Dragon was going to reach Michelle's group before they were able to distract it.

"Yeah!" yelled Bryan between swings of his scimitars. "We need to get to the Dragon, now! Ideas?"

Peter had been hoping Bryan had an idea. They were about as far from the Dragon as they were from Michelle's group, and the Dragon had decided to zero in on Michelle's group instead of Peter and Bryan. Either they needed to find a way to get the Dragon's attention from afar, or they needed to intercept it before it got to Michelle's group, who would be trampled or forced to break rank. Of course, Peter had no idea how he and Bryan were going to fare any better with the giant beast, but at least they had volunteered to do it.

They needed to do something fast.

"No ideas here," called the closest Peter to Bryan. "You?"

"Nope," said Bryan. "But we need to move faster!"

"Ok, so let's move faster."

"Trying!" said Bryan. "It just all these little green things in the way."

"Yeah, it's almost like they don't appreciate being cut to ribbons!" said Peter.

The Dragon was almost halfway to Michelle's group now. They would have to sprint to get to the beast in time.

"Screw it," said Peter. "Let's just go!"

All five of the Peters broke out of their loose, circular formation and started sprinting to the Dragon through the sea of green little men with rusty swords. They formed a tight, flying "V" formation, while Bryan took up the chase fitting right in the center of the V with his chainmail ringing with every step. With their six-foot-four, two-hundred-pound frames, the five Peters didn't have any problems keeping a sprinting pace through the much lighter and shorter Goblins. Judging by the first few he threw aside with an appropriately placed shoulder check, he figured they couldn't weigh much more than forty pounds each.

The problem was that each of these super-bantamweight thugs had sharp weapons, which made charging into them similar to running through a gauntlet of razor blades. The lead Peter was cut deeply on the right side of his face by a Goblin sword and slowed the pace of the rest of them considerably. Suddenly, they were all bleeding.

The shock of their charge had worn off, and now the Goblins were turning to meet them with raised swords. They were no longer running through a sea of surprised armed little men. They were running through a sea of *prepared* armed little men.

The Peter acting as the point for the group took the worst of it. His two Trow swords looked like pinwheels for all the parrying and slashing they did. He wasn't trying to kill or even hit the Goblins. His entire purpose and focus was moving through the crowd as quickly as possible and, in a few cases, this meant accepting blows he could have avoided by slowing down.

They were about a hundred feet from the charging Dragon when the lead Peter's foot caught in the loose leather armor of a Goblin he had stepped on to maintain speed. He tucked into a roll, plowing into a line of Goblins. Luckily, they had expected him to jump and had their weapons raised high so that when he bowled into them he avoided being skewered.

Peter had to make a split-second decision. With one of the Peters tangled up on the ground, they either had to slow down and help him recover, which would cause them to miss their chance to intercept the Dragon, or leave him behind in the middle of a sea of Goblins, which was as good as a death sentence.

There wasn't a choice to be made. The Dragon needed to be stopped. He left one Peter behind to help the fallen one and continued on with the remaining three.

Bryan hesitated for a half-step, then continued with the group of three Peters, understanding the decision that had been made. Peter's consciousness was now split between three different areas: one of him was helping Billy and Erin to exact the other part of their hackneyed plan, two of him were now standing back to back defending themselves as best they could in the sea of Goblins, and the remaining three were racing towards a Dragon in an effort to keep it away from Michelle's group. It should have felt confusing, but it didn't. Experiencing the same reality in these three different ways was enhancing, if not exhilarating.

Could this be what enlightenment was like?

Bryan's heavy chain mail armor was coming into good use as he moved to the front and led the charge. The Peters tapered out on either side of him. They must have looked like a small group of Canadian geese.

As Bryan ran, the lower portion of the mail bounced against his knees, giving the same cadence and tinkling beat one would expect from a Christmas sleigh ride. Peter tried to imagine how the weight of the armor felt on Bryan's shoulders, how the leather belt kept the chainmail tight against his stomach, how vibrations of impact would conduct through his two scimitars when striking true.

He felt an overwhelming, familiar pressure building within his mind. As before, it wasn't *in* his head per say. It had nothing to do with his physical body. It was mental pressure and, as before, it was released with an expansive mental explosion.

Bryan's senses were now his own.

He could feel each step Bryan took in his heavy steel-toed boots, each step offering the potential of a turned ankle on the uneven forest floor. He could feel how there were a few open rings of the chain mail near the back of the armor that rubbed his left leg irritatingly every few steps. But more importantly, Peter was able to link Bryan's senses with his own and this allowed him to see where each step and each swing of the scimitar would take them.

Suddenly, the Peters on either side of Bryan started swinging in concert with him. Bryan would send a Goblin to the ground on the left of him with a powerful jab and the Peter on the right of him would complement Bryan's movement by moving up a half-step to protect his exposed flank. At the same time, the Peter on the left would shift his position to allow Bryan to complete his swing unabated. The adjustments were the smallest imperceptible shifts in timing and position of the group, but they made all the difference. They gained speed.

They were going to make it and Peter could sense a shift in Bryan's gait. He was adjusting for the collision with the Dragon, except, instead of pulling up, he was lengthening his stride. He was adjusting for something, and, just as they closed the final few steps, Peter realized what he was planning. The Dragon turned their way.

"Bryan! Don't do it!" shouted the two Peter's on either side of him.

But it was too late. Bryan closed the last two steps on the Dragon and leapt in the air. His jump was perfectly timed and, as the Dragon turned its mattress-sized head their way, Bryan brought is sword down hard. The Dragon's head snaked lightning fast away from the blow, so instead of being run through, the Dragon received a hearty blow to the lower jaw from Bryan's mail-cladded fist. Peter saw the Dragon's head recoil from the blow as Bryan landed on the far side, placing the monster between himself and the Peters.

"Did you just punch the Dragon in the mouth?" asked Peter in disbelief.

Bryan turned and flashed a wide smile to the Peters. "Yes. Yes I sure did."

A concussive roar made Bryan and the Peters brace themselves, so as to not lose their footing. The nearby Goblins collapsed to the ground from the physical impact of the Dragon's rage-filled battle cry. Peter could feel thick waves of fury rolling within the dark beast. It was focused on Bryan.

"Mission accomplished!" said Bryan with another flash of a smile, before he sprinted back up the trail from where the Dragon had come. The mountain of scales, teeth and fury followed behind.

CHAPTER 19

The entire battlefield drew back as the Dragon exploded in rage. Somehow, she had forgotten about the Dragon. Bryan and Peter were supposed to distract it before Michelle and the rest were flattened or flambéed by it. She strained to see over the group and saw the beast racing back up the hill from where it came. She could see the Peters running after the Dragon but couldn't see where Bryan was. It looked like the Dragon was running away from the group of three Peters, but that didn't seem right.

She brought her attention back to the battle. Bryan and Peter needed to do their part and she was going to do hers. She figured she had rested for at least two minutes and was ready to give someone else a break. She licked her dry lips wishing they had brought water.

"Who needs a break?" she asked the four in front of her.

"I could use one," said Jenn without turning.

Michelle watched as Jenn brought her two-handed battle-axe down onto two ill-prepared Goblins. She noted that Jenn and Judd both had settled on similar highly-effective tactics and weapons and wondered if it reflected a personality match.

She positioned herself behind Jenn and prepared for the switch. Jenn held a wide stance to support her heavy swings and Michelle chose her position carefully to not get in the way. She looked out over the sea of Goblins wondering how long they could survive. The Goblins didn't seem to be concerned with their lives. They just kept on coming. She noticed a few Goblins climbing trees a few-hundred feet away, and scanned the canopy blanketing their position. She didn't see anything. Judd and Billy had described how the Trow had used any means possible to ambush them. They should have been on the lookout for things like that, but she didn't see anything in the trees near them.

"There are a bunch of Goblins climbing trees back there," she called out. "I don't know what they are doing, but we shouldn't assume they are going to be satisfied with this stalemate."

Michelle saw Marci stiffen and jerk her head around, looking in the trees above.

"I checked. They aren't above us," said Michelle. "They tried to drop trees on the Ogres a while back."

"Those trees are too far away. And besides, why would they climb trees they are going to cut down? They are climbing up pretty high," said Marci.

"Perhaps they are just trying to get a better view," called Judd over the cacophony.

"And . . . switch!" yelled Jenn as she stepped away from the battle.

Michelle was caught off guard and scrambled to fill the void. A few Goblins noticed the opportunity and rushed her position, but Michelle made quick work of them with her two swords.

Jenn called from the center of the group, "That cannot be good news. Does anyone have water? Or better yet how about some wine? Does anyone have wine?"

"They are doing something," called Judd. "Something is coming."

Michelle couldn't see much beyond the few Goblins in front of her. She looked up where the Goblins had been climbing and could see groups of them packed together at the tops of very tall trees. She thought she could see ropes or chains dangling down from where they stood. Something flew over her head impacting the ground behind her. A chain landed on her shoulder and she instinctively brushed it off as if it were a spider. She heard several other thuds and saw chains leading back into the Goblin horde.

"Son of a mother!" Jenn screamed from the center. "That hurts!"

Michelle looked up at the trees again and saw the groups of Goblins jump from the tops of the trees and dangle from chains as they descended. The chain she had brushed off her shoulder pulled taught and she heard screams of pain from her group. Suddenly her legs were kicked out from under her from behind as something barreled through her.

It was Jenn! Michelle watched in horror as Jenn was pulled at high speed away from the group and into the Goblin horde. Just before she disappeared, Michelle saw through the kicked-up dirt and leaves what looked like a three-sided grappling hook lodged deeply into Jenn's thigh.

"Jenn!" yelled Michelle after her.

She looked to the group and saw that at least two others had been pulled away. Judd, reacting to Michelle's call, looked over in time to see his wife disappear. She saw his face grow hard and he charged into the Goblins, following in Jenn's wake.

"Keep this group alive!" Michelle called out to Marci as she raced after Judd and Jenn.

Marci took a step back to close the circle tighter and stepped on something solid. She looked down to see Jenn's double-bladed battle-axe.

CHAPTER 20

The three Peters ran after the Dragon focused on Bryan. Their job had been to pull the Dragon away from the larger group and things were going quite well in that department. The kerfuffle in all of this was that Peter and Bryan hadn't talked about what they were going to *do* once they got the Dragon's attention or, more specifically, how they were going to stay alive once they had it.

Going toe-to-toe with a Dragon had been something he'd dreamed about ever since he read the *Dungeons and Dragons* novels in elementary school. He had read nearly every *Forgotten Realms* series that existed, and every time a character battled with a Dragon it resulted in either a clever trick allowing the hero to win or escape, or the Dragon lived up to its reputation and ended things with a meal.

Of course, in his teenage mind's eye, in the unlikely event that he ever battled a Dragon, either he would prevail with the same spunky ploys his storybook heroes employed, or if he did meet his demise, it would be a sacrifice for the ages. Perhaps his arm or leg would have been removed, but it all would have been worth it to save a boatload of blind, toddler orphans or perhaps a ravishing group of Brazilian bikini models from which he would accept no rewards other than their gratitude due to his unremitting moral compass.

That was how Dragon battles were supposed to go. It was supposed to be bold, flashy and courageous, and preferably with bikini models. Instead, he found himself chasing after a Dragon that was trying to roast his friend in theatre chainmail. Where was the moxy in that?

He supposed Bryan had done a good job distributing the moxy when he clocked the Dragon in the chin. But now the multi-ton lizard beast was running him down, and when it caught him Peter didn't expect things to go well.

Except the Dragon didn't seem to be catching up with Bryan. In fact, Peter had to slow down a few times to not bump into its tail. It was moving fast enough, but it was a pace that the Peters didn't have difficulty matching.

Peter had a hard time believing that the Dragon was pacing itself in some way. He was sure there was no calm rational physical resource-rationing in play here. So why was it so easy to keep up with the thing? They were running uphill, following the path, presumably toward the cave entrance where it had emerged. Bryan had wisely chosen to stay on the path. If he stayed on the path, he would be presented with a predictable, if not wholly uniform, running surface, whereas bolting through the forest was just asking for a turned ankle or an unfortunate interaction with trip-inducing sticks and logs. Luckily, the thing just wasn't all that fast, which was surprising. And, if Peter was being honest with himself, a little upsetting.

He'd expected the thing to be lightning quick. Sure, it was massive, and it took a lot of force to move something that large, but somehow it didn't seem right that it wasn't faster. In *Jurassic Park*, the T-Rex had nearly caught a Jeep going forty miles per hour. He remembered the camera flashing to the speedometer as if the director was saying "look how fast this thing is!" Of course, the top running speed of a dinosaur fifty-million years extinct was pure conjecture. The Dragon had a body-type similar to Komodo Dragon, which he knew were known for ambushing their victims. They would take a single devastating bite, allow them to run away, then follow the trail of blood to where its victim had succumbed to its blight-laden bite.

It was also odd that the Dragon didn't toast Bryan with flame and end all this silly chasing. It certainly was a fire-breathing Dragon, he had seen as much when it projected a rave-quality light show a few-hundred feet into the air. Maybe it needed recovery time between plumes of fire. Either way, it didn't matter. Somehow, Bryan was still alive despite the Dragon's best efforts.

Running, however, was a temporary solution. Either Bryan would tire out and need to face the Dragon toe to claw, or the Dragon would lose steam and turn around and go back to exactly where they didn't want it to go. They needed a way to neutralize the beast.

Peter didn't see any blind toddler orphans, so the noble sacrifice thing seemed to be out the window. He needed a clever plan. He was probably overqualified for battling Dragons if reading fantasy novels counted for anything. He just needed to go down the list.

He didn't have a long iron arrow and even if he did, this Dragon wasn't flying, and he didn't have a way to shoot it. This Dragon didn't seem to talk and the time for clever verbal bluffs had long passed. He didn't have any explosives to throw in its mouth the second before it breathed fire. He didn't have much.

He needed to think about what he did have. His family beat the large Screecher didn't they? The Dragon wasn't much bigger and a lot slower, and they hadn't been prepared in their tousle with the Screecher either. Of course, it had taken a car and a gas fire to defeat that one, but Peter figured fire wasn't going to help here.

They had beaten the Ogres, sort of. His son had taken care of that one. He wished they hadn't sent the Ogres away. This was their kind of job; brutal weight and muscle work.

That's it! Ha! Not quite a clever plan, but it will have to do.

He called above the thunderous steps of the Dragon. "Bryan! Go to the cave! We need to be near the cave!"

Bryan called back, out of breath, "W – where . . . is . . . that?"

Right.

The old man knew where it was. They didn't. It was somewhere up in the hills, but that was about all Peter knew.

"The bad guys all came from the cave! When you see a beaten path off the trail, take it!" he called back.

"Right!"

It didn't take long; Bryan took a sharp right into the wood a few minutes later. The Dragon slammed into a few pine trees trying to make the turn, sending splinters flying and trees toppling. They ran along the trail for a minute or two.

Bryan called back, sweating his full bodyweight through the chainmail. "Okay! . . . Now what?"

Peter called out, "Help, Help, Help!"

"That's the plan?"

"Yup. Help!"

Bryan joined in. "Help!"

The Dragon snorted what Peter interpreted as a smug laugh. It was cut short when a freight train of power and muscle plowed into it its side, sending them both half a football field from the path.

"Watch out!" Peter called out as the trees fell in their wake.

Bryan and the three Peters scattered. Peter turned to see the Dragon right itself and turn to face its new foe. The Ogre rolled its shoulders and crouched low ready for the battle.

"Where did he come from?" asked Bryan.

"We sent one with the kids," said Peter, grinning to himself.

The Dragon charged the Ogre, mouth open revealing its razor-sharp teeth. The Ogre shot out towards the Dragon to meet it and the two collided in a thunderclap.

CHAPTER 21

Michelle raced after Judd. He was barreling through the Goblins trying to get to Jenn. Michelle could see that, even though he kept swinging his holy water sprinkler, he was taking significant damage as he went. It was one thing to hold a line against two or three Goblins at a time; it was quite another to charge through hundreds of them by yourself. She saw him stumble once or twice as he took deep cuts to his legs.

The man was a giant compared to the Goblins. He was a lot closer to seven-feet tall than six, which meant that Judd was running through the Goblins like a tornado runs through a trailer park. It also meant that just about all of the blows he sustained were from the waist down, and blood ran down his legs from a few nasty gashes.

She didn't doubt that he would get to Jenn. What concerned her was what he would find when he got there and how long he would survive after arriving. What looked like a three-sided fishhook had been deeply lodged in Jenn's thigh, attached to a chain that had dragged her away. Michelle had warned them about the Goblins climbing trees, but it wasn't until Jenn had been dragged away that they understood why.

Michelle didn't immediately follow Judd. She had to solidify the group before she could leave them down three people, and, once she was satisfied they could handle themselves, she took off into a sprint.

"I am fast. I am strong!" The stone burned in her hand as she drew upon its power. Her steps came faster, and her sword arm became a blur of motion. Soon, she caught up with Judd and took a position on his left. He didn't seem to notice her presence and continued his bull rush.

"Jenn!" called Judd as he ran. "I'm coming!"

Michelle bit her lip. Jenn was alone, hurt, surrounded and weaponless. There was a good chance they wouldn't like what they would find.

"Judd . . ." Michelle began. "I don't think –"

"Jenn!" he yelled again.

Michelle gave up trying to talk to Judd and did her best to keep them both alive.

"I am fast. I am strong!" she said as she ran her sword through another Goblin.

Judd stopped amid the battle, Goblins all around. His gaze was fixed a few yards ahead, and Michelle cringed to think what he was seeing. She knew what they would find. She sliced through a few Goblins in front of them, hoping to buy a moment so that she could talk him back to the group, to tell him that his children needed him alive. But when the Goblins dropped she fell into the same shock that Judd had.

There stood Jenn leaning on her right foot, her left bathed in blood from hip to ankle, swinging the three-sided hook over her head by the very chain that had dragged her away. She had managed to clear herself a space of about five feet around her.

"Come on, ya little green freaks!" Jenn yelled as she swung the hook out at a group of Goblins, testing the distance between them. "Gonna take more than that to take me down!"

As she swung, Jenn let out more of the chain and caught one of the Goblins in the throat. The hook sunk deep as Jenn pulled back sharply, and that was when the cowards charged, seeing that her weapon was no longer available. Judd stepped in swinging his holy water sprinkler and Michelle followed.

"I was sure you were dead," said Michelle to Jenn.

"Nope. Just fishing," answered Jenn as she slammed the Goblin she caught into the ground. It lay motionless.

"Any bites?" asked Judd, the sound of worry slowly dropping from his deep voice.

"A few," said Jenn pulling her hook from the Goblins. "But no keepers".

"Your leg doesn't look good and you've lost a lot of blood. Your whole leg is soaked. We have to move," said Michelle. "Judd, take over for a sec."

Jenn looked down at her leg and seemed to notice the blood for the first time. She slumped over as Judd adjusted his tactic to wide horizontal swings to keep the Goblins at bay. Michelle tore off a sleeve of her shirt and wrapped a makeshift tourniquet around her leg, stemming some of the bleeding.

But then she looked at Judd and didn't understand how the man was still fighting. All up and down his legs were deep angry cuts. She could see slashes that and been so deep and angled that the skin now flapped like a loose fish gill. His legs were wet with red blood. The thought of their children felt like a heavy weight pressing down on Michelle's shoulders. How was she going to keep them alive?

"Judd, sit down beside Jenn. You've lost too much blood to fight," she said, pulling him back and engaging the wary Goblins. "You're cut up pretty bad, both of you."

Michelle spun around them in lightning-quick circles, her blade flashing. She was able to keep the Goblins at bay, but that wasn't going to get Judd and Jenn back to the group. She couldn't do this all day. In fact, she was starting to get tired.

How long had she been fighting? No one could fight forever. She missed a step and a rusty Goblin blade just missed her eye socket by a few inches. She felt the rock growing cold in her hand and realized what she had done.

The old man had warned her about this. Her stone would respond to her thoughts.

I am fast. I am strong.

She continued sweeping the circle around Jenn and Judd, keeping the Goblins away. She needed to move them, but they could barely stand now that she'd told them to withdraw.

I should have kept my mouth shut. Now they can barely move. If only they had a stone . . .

She felt the stone going cold in her hands again, but this time it wasn't responding to her. It was responding to something else, projecting. Then she remembered the old man in the basement, trying to make her laugh. He'd gotten a few out of her, but at the time she didn't know what he was trying to say to her, cryptic little bugger. Now she knew.

I can rally them back to standing. I have to get them standing, or we're all done for.

"Judd and Jenn!" she called as she spun around them in a circle. "Get up! You are stronger than that!" They groaned in response. "Jenn, didn't you tell me you moved the swing set all by yourself when you heard Judd wasn't going to be home that night? And Judd, you are gargantuan! It would take an elephant gun to bring you down. Get up, you bums!"

She kept on them as she circled around slashing at the Goblins, "You had four kids, Jenn. This is waaaay easier than that! And Judd you're married to Jenn, that's gotta count for something in the rugged department."

Michelle squeezed her stone in her left hand using the tips of her fingers to press it into her palm, her nails pushing into its hard, smooth surface. As she harassed them, the stone shifted from warm to white hot. She held fast. She could smell smoke seeping through her fingers. She had lost all feeling in her fingertips.

She heard Judd groan as he got to his feet. "Do you suppose she will quit her yapping if we get up?"

"I'll try anything at this point. It's worse than getting hooked by the Goblins," Jenn replied.

"You both are *strong,* and you will be stronger for your children. We will get out of this for them," said Michelle.

Judd raised an eyebrow at Michelle then took a step forward and leveled a mighty swing of his six-foot holy water sprinkler into the first row of Goblins. Michelle heard a sickening cracking noise like someone stepping on dry twigs upon the impact. The blow launched two rows of Goblins back into the rank and file like cannon fodder into wet paper. He leveled at least ten Goblins with a single blow.

Jenn slapped him on the back and said, "Nice, honey! My turn!"

She whipped the hook around her head in a short circle and sent it flying into the Goblins. She hooked one, pulled it back, confirmed it wasn't going anywhere, gave the chain a bit of slack and whipped the creature back into the horde, toppling five or six more. She yanked hard on the hook and it came back to her mostly Goblin-free, save for a few small pieces. She caught the base of the three-sided hook like a yo-yo, held it up for them to see, and licked the edge of one of the hook blades.

"That is so badass!" said Judd. Michelle squirmed.

Jenn held the pose for half-a-second then her face turned sour. She started spitting everything from her mouth, and then the dry-heaving started.

"Don't . . ." said Jenn between spits, ". . . don't let me do that again. Super-gross."

Together they had cleared close to twenty Goblins. The stone was doing its work. "Yeesh, guys," said Michelle, "Keep this up and we won't even need Billy and Erin. Let's get back to the rest of the group. I think I have something to say to them."

Judd took two quick steps and swung an opening in the direction of the bridge. He gestured a short bow and swept his open palm, indicating his southern gentlemanly adherence to the principle of "ladies first".

"That was wretched! Ugh," said Jenn, still spitting as they made their way back to the bridge. "I think I got some eyeball between my teeth!"

CHAPTER 22

Bryan and Peter were forced back by the percussive shock wave created when the two titans met. Tress toppled like bowling pins creating a thunderstorm of dust and noise. Though they were a safe distance away, both Peter and Bryan crouched behind thick pine trees. As the dust started to clear they could see the shadowy bulk of the Ogre circling around the coiled form of the Dragon.

The Ogre darted in, swinging hard with its meaty tire-sized fist, punching the Dragon in the gizzard. Again, dust flew in a rolling puff when the Dragon dropped to the ground. The Ogre leapt to its feet ready to deliver a two-fisted blow to the Dragon's head only to have the Dragon pop up as soon as the Ogre left its feet.

Peter winced. Once you leave your feet it is impossible to change direction. The Dragon took full advantage of the Ogres mistake and struck out with jaws gaping. It latched onto the forearm of the Ogre and pulled hard. The Ogre's arm snapped like a dry twig. Peter could see that it was sticking out of the Dragon's mouth at an odd angle. The Ogre pulled hard on its now broken forearm bringing in the Dragon closer. Then it used its other arm to deliver a devastating uppercut to the Dragon's throat sending the fire-breathing beast barreling through pine trees older than Peter's grandfather.

"So . . . now what?" asked Bryan, sitting down, back up against a fallen log.

"I'm not sure," answered Peter. "Hey where the heck did you get the popcorn?"

"It's been dangling around in my greaves all afternoon. Must've been from the last renaissance fair," he said, chomping on a handful of squished popcorn. "And what do you mean you don't know what to do next? You're the one who told me to come this way."

"Yea. I figured if we found the Ogre he would help."

"And he is, but who is going to help him?" asked Bryan.

They watched the Ogre and Dragon circle each other. The Dragon lunged with a snake-like strike only to have the Ogre jump just out of reach, toppling yet another tree.

"This isn't good for the forest," commented Bryan, throwing another kernel in his mouth. "I wonder. Why doesn't the Dragon breathe fire?"

"Weird, right? I mean, not that I want the Ogre roasted," answered Peter. "We need to find a way to help. I don't know if our boy is going to get the upper hand here."

"Do we have to help? We could just wait for Billy and Erin to do their part, couldn't we?"

"Yeah, but the Ogre would be stuck here. If we close the bridges, the Goblins and the Dragon will group up on him. He probably wouldn't make it, Bryan," said Peter. He was starting to get a little attached to these big brutes.

The Dragon lunged again, but this time it swung its tail around and landed a solid blow. The Ogre roared and flew backward, smashing through pines as thick as car tires. The Dragon charged the fallen Ogre, and Peter was relieved to see it regain its feet just in time to avoid the Dragon's snapping jaws.

"Okay, we really need a plan," said Peter holding his right elbow in his left hand and placing his right hand on his temple. "Think. Think. Think."

"You sound like Winnie the Pooh," observed Bryan.

"And you sound like my kids."

The Ogre grabbed a toppled tree and broke the thick log on the Dragon's back. However, the powerful strike didn't slow the Dragon, and it smashed through the log and snapped at the Ogre, forcing it to retreat.

Bryan whistled low, "I'm not sure we can do anything to help. If the Dragon can shake off a blow like that, we wouldn't be anything more than annoying gnats."

"Annoying enough to chase," added Peter with a smile. "We're pretty good at that, aren't we?"

The Dragon swung its tail, trying to catch the Ogre off-guard again, but this time the Ogre wised up and caught its tail. To their amazement, the Ogre started dragging the beast through the forest as it rolled and tried to double back on itself to snap at him. But the Ogre was moving too quickly.

"Now what is it doing?" Peter asked Bryan as they followed at a safe distance.

The Ogre continued to drag the squirming, twisting Dragon through the woods. Then Peter realized where the Ogre was taking it.

"I wonder . . ." said Peter, staring at a large crack in the earth. "Bryan, this must be the cave entrance! He must be trying to send the Dragon back in the cave!"

"How does that help?" asked Bryan,

"Hmm, no clue," said Peter.

The Dragon scrambled and tore at the earth as the Ogre spun it around, but it couldn't find purchase enough to slow its momentum. With a great heave, the Ogre let go, and the Dragon flew into the crack, disappearing into its grey black mouth. Peter counted two seconds until he heard it hit the ground in a solid thud.

"About fifty feet," said Peter.

"What?" asked Bryan.

"It fell for about two seconds so that should be about fifty, maybe sixty, feet," said Peter. "The Ogre just threw it off a cliff, an underground cliff. Sixty feet is a long way down and that thing had to weigh more than ten tons. It hit hard, hopefully on a bunch of stalagmites."

Peter watched as the Ogre stood still twenty feet from the cave entrance. Something about the way it stood unnerved him.

It took him a second to realize that the thing wasn't breathing heavily. It had just been in a life or death struggle with a *Dragon* and it wasn't out of breath. In fact, Peter was breathing heavier than the Ogre just from the excitement of watching the fight. He reminded himself how lucky they were that the Ogres were on their side.

A fierce roar preceded the Dragon's reappearance at the cave mouth. The way it scrambled out of the cave reminded Peter of a gecko he and Michelle were visited by on their honeymoon in Australia. There was no sign of injury and, if anything, the Dragon looked even more limber coming out of its home territory. The Ogre crouched in an athletic pose, readying itself for the next attack, when the Dragon's eyes suddenly got wide. It clawed at the ground, pulling deep gashes into the clay and soil of the forest. Despite using all four of its powerful legs, it was moving backwards into the cave.

The Dragon let out another roar, this time sounding less like a challenge and more like a plea for help just before it disappeared into the cave. Peter counted to himself listening for the impact. He got to seven before he heard a thud.

Turning to Bryan he said, "That doesn't make sense. The first time it was two seconds and now seven?"

Bryan pointed to the cave mouth and took two steps backward. "Peter, I don't think that sound was the Dragon hitting the bottom of the cave. Look."

Near the cave entrance sat the lifeless head of the Dragon. A second later Peter heard something loud echo from within, and he froze, his body reacting faster than his mind. Something was very wrong. His body knew it, but his mind was still catching up. Something in the cave had killed the Dragon and thrown its head back out. That was chilling enough, but that wasn't what had him frozen.

What was the second thud?

It must have been the body of the Dragon. Whatever had killed the Dragon had decapitated it, thrown the head over the edge, then dropped its body down to the cave floor. This meant that it was both impossibly strong and large, and, worse yet, that it was at the mouth of the cave, only feet from where they were standing.

Peter focused in on the darkness of the cave, straining to see anything. He thought he saw movement. Not movement that would suggest specific form, but a shift of the darkness itself.

"This is bad," said Peter under his breath. The hair was standing up on the back of his neck. "This is very bad. We need to go, Bryan. Now."

"I agree," said Bryan.

Before they moved a muscle, the cave entrance exploded outward, throwing boulder sized rocks in every direction. Peter and Bryan didn't turn to see what was coming. It didn't matter what it was. It was time to run.

A cannon shot sound came from behind them and they saw the Ogre fly up and out over the forest like an ambitious bottle rocket. "Definitely not good," said Peter, racing for his life down the trail with Bryan. "I suddenly miss the Dragon."

CHAPTER 23

"Guys, that's not going to work," said Brad.

He was standing with one foot on a large, moss-covered rock that contributed to the east bank of the stream. He was looking up at the three-foot diameter concrete tube that linked the lake on the far side of the earthen levee to the small stream that continued through the forest behind him. Billy climbed out of the tunnel trying to shake off his water-soaked pants.

"You could have said something *before* I climbed in the tunnel," said Billy.

"It's called a culvert and it's made out of concrete," said Brad.

Billy's feet were soaked. He hated wet socks. Billy was going to punch him if he did that smile of his. He took a few steps closer, hoping to be within arm's reach just in case.

"What do you mean it won't work?" asked Erin, putting an arm on Billy's shoulder. "All the tanks are in the tube. When we blow up the tanks, it will blow a hole in the levee and flood the stream and everything around it. There should be more than enough water in the lake to wash out any dams they have made."

"How are you going to explode the tanks?" asked Brad.

"Billy will shoot them. He's a pretty good shot," said Peter from the other side of the stream, "A nice hot bullet ripping through the tanks should definitely make them blow."

Brad shook his head. "Think about it. This long concrete culvert is like a rifle barrel. If you cause an explosion in the middle, it will just shoot the explosion out the end like a gunshot. It won't blow up the levee."

"So we have the Ogre smash both ends plugging them, then blow it up," said Peter.

"How do you ignite it if both ends are smashed closed," asked Brad.

Peter opened his mouth as if to say something then closed it. "Crap," he said.

They all stood there in silence. Billy swatted at a mosquito. He hated to admit it, but he was sure it had to be sealed to in order to actually blow the thing up.

"How sure are you that we can't just have Billy shoot it without plugging it up?" asked Peter. "I've been to mines in Pennsylvania and they drill and blast to bring down rock. They don't plug up the holes before blasting."

"Was it coal?" asked Brad.

"Yea," said Peter.

"Coal is like a wet noodle compared to high-strength silica fume concrete. I'm telling you if you don't plug the tube the explosion will just come out either end," said Brad.

Billy turned to Peter. "What does he do again?"

"He builds some crazy pools. He's won national titles," said Peter.

"High end pools with a lot of concrete," added Brad. Again, they all looked at the propane tank filled concrete tube in silence. "Why don't you just have the Ogre dig through the levee? He looks strong enough."

"He can't cross running water. As soon as any water starts flowing, he will be blown back. He could probably get some more water going, but we need to create a flash flood to wash away the dams," said Peter.

"How are the others?" asked Erin.

They could all hear the battle in the forest. They were less than a mile from where the others were fighting the Goblins and the Dragon, trying to keep them from crossing the streambed.

Peter answered without hesitation, "They're doing okay. Bryan and Peter led the Dragon away from the rest of them and into an introduction with an Ogre. It is a stalemate right now. We should not assume it will stay that way though. They are going to get tired."

"Okay, we can figure this out," said Brad.

"We had this figured out until you showed up," said Billy under his breath.

"If we smash down both sides of the tube, it will blow the levee like you want it to. The trick is igniting it. We need a way to ignite it remotely," said Brad, ignoring Billy.

"Hey, how about a cell phone?" asked Erin. "Don't they have warning signs up around gas stations saying you might cause a fire by using a cell phone?"

"That they do," said Peter.

"We could throw a cell phone in there and then call it after the Ogre smashes down the sides of the tube," said Brad.

"I've seen the signs, but I don't think it would work," said Peter shaking his head. "The phone doesn't make sparks or anything. How many times have you used your phone at a gas station? I think everyone does it, and you never hear about a fire because of it."

"This is a lot of talking and not a lot of doing. Our friends are right over there fighting for their lives, for our lives, and we are chatting about cell phones," said Billy getting frustrated.

"Okay, okay," said Peter. "We can try the cell phone thing, but let's push the odds in our favor. We can break the glass covering for the light and set the picture timer to have the flash go off. That might make a spark."

After a minute or two of discussing whose phone was the most appropriate for sacrifice, it was decided that Billy's phone would be the one to use. The other's either weren't working or had bad reception. Erin had a phone, so Billy's was deemed superfluous. That and he had the best replacement plan of them all.

They had the Ogre smash the lakeside of the tube first to cut off any water flow. Then they were ready to execute the plan. Billy crawled into the tube again and opened up a tank to let out some propane. Nothing happened.

"These things have a check valve or something! I opened the tank, but the gas isn't coming out!" he shouted. "I'm going to have to shoot one open from out there."

When Billy got out of the tube, they arranged themselves around it.

"Okay," said Billy. "I'll shoot the tank to get the gas flowing. If it doesn't blow up, then Peter throws in the phone with the picture timer going. As soon as Peter throws the phone, the Ogre smashes closed the tube. Got it?"

They all nodded in the affirmative. Billy positioned himself in front of the tube back a few yards so that he could get a good shot. Peter crouched low on the left side and the Ogre was on the right. Billy brought his rifle to his cheek, took aim and shot.

"Did you hit it?" asked Peter.

"Of course I hit it," said Billy. "Throw it in!"

Peter threw in the phone and as planned, the Ogre smashed down the end of the tube, shoving the broken material back up into the culvert to create a good seal. As the Ogre was doing his part, Peter and Billy scrambled away from the tube to a spot about fifty feet away, where Erin, Brad and Catherine were hiding behind a thick tree. Peter made sure that he could hear the Ogre following after they took a few steps. He didn't want the Ogre to be blasted by magical force of the rushing water and he wanted to make sure that it wasn't stuck on the wrong side of the stream once washed out the dams. The Ogre joined them a few seconds after Peter and Billy arrived. They waited in pregnant silence for half a minute.

Billy was the first to break the silence, "You set the picture timer before you threw it in right?"

Peter took a deep breath and sighed. "Crap! No. Sorry."

"I am *not* going in that tube for a third time," said Billy.

"Culvert. It's a *culvert*," said Brad.

Peter and the rest looked up when they saw something plummet across the sky and then generate a loud splash in the lake. They couldn't see the lake from where they stood below the levee, but Peter knew what it was.

"That was an Ogre . . . we need to blow the levee *now*," said Peter. "There is something very bad coming out of the deeps."

"Yeah we know," said Erin. "You told us. The Dragon . . ."

"No," interrupted Peter. "Whatever just came out killed the Dragon and convinced an Ogre to do his best impression of a firework."

"So you saw what it was?" asked Erin. "The "other you" saw it?"

"No. He just ran."

Billy muttered under his breath something about that being first sensible thing they had done all day.

"Here," offered Erin. "I'll text the phone. That might work. Right?"

CHAPTER 24

"What the heck is that thing?" yelled Bryan as he and the three Peters bolted down the trail.

"I don't know," Peter called back. "I didn't look."

"Me neither! I figured you were going to with there being three of you and all."

They were running down the hill choosing to cut across the woods where the trail turned back on itself. It was the fastest and most hazardous way to get back to the bridge, but considering what was behind them, it seemed appropriate.

Peter had seen movement coming from the deep crack in the ground, but he hadn't been able to make anything out. When the crack exploded outward, he instinctively ran for his life.

Judging by what had happened to the Ogre, he was comfortable with that decision.

Whatever was behind them had manhandled the Ogre and ended the Dragon before they even realized what was happening. Their only hope was to get away from the thing as quickly as possible, and that meant running like spooked deer through the woods. Peter arranged the three of him around Bryan so that one of him was in front and two more were on each side of him, allowing Peter to use his six eyes to track the unpredictable ground conditions.

Peter knew through the other Peters that the dams had not been breached, and he couldn't count on it happening any time soon. The two Peter's were still fighting for their lives in the Goblin horde, so he had no idea how Michelle's group was fairing. He could only hope for the best and pray that his wife and friends were okay.

"Argh!" Peter yelled at himself.

"What?" asked Bryan, hopping over a low thorny bush.

"We can't run back to the group. We would just bring this thing down on them," said Peter.

"Oh, yeah," said Bryan, looking back. "Yeah, we need to run down a different way. But, to be honest, I'm not even sure we are being chased."

Peter glanced behind his shoulder, trusting the vision of his other two selves to keep him from tripping. There was nothing but forest. There were plenty of trees, but nothing large and hideous chasing them. He slowed his pace for a few strides, taking a closer look, and then stopped. Bryan did the same.

The four of them stood facing the direction they had come, breathing heavily. All four of them were sopping wet with sweat. Peter felt a weak breeze dance across them and it was like manna from heaven. They were hot and tired. And nothing was chasing them.

"I'm confused," said Peter. "I mean, kind of relieved. But confused."

"Me too."

Peter caught himself unconsciously wiping the green-brown Goblin blood off his blade as they watched the woods. It seemed an odd thing to do. He must have picked it up from movies. Movie heroes always wiped blood off of their blades after using them. But Peter didn't really feel like a hero.

He and Bryan had dreamed of doing something like this their entire lives. In Peter's case, it had been ever since he started reading fantasy novels as a pre-teen. Back in high school, he didn't start working out every day to be healthy or even to look good for the ladies. He wanted to be strong like the blacksmiths in his stories.

They always seemed to grow up to be devastatingly powerful warriors that fought for the good in the world. He hadn't studied physics and chemistry to get a good job. They were the closest subjects in school to being an honest-to-gosh wizard. He had been waiting for a reason to use his strength and wizard-like powers to strike virtuous blows since he was thirteen. Before they had kids, when he and Michelle would walk down the street in Manhattan, he had almost wanted someone to take her purse because it would finally give him the perfect excuse to prove how mighty he was or at least how mighty he thought he was.

After the kids had been born, the daydreams became grander. Perhaps someone would grab a kid from the front yard on his watch. The perpetrator would jump in a car and step on the gas assuming the deed was done, but Peter had been ready. He had trained. He had planned. And he had the righteous power of a furious dad protecting his brood. The car would have to stay on the road. Peter wouldn't. He would cut across the back yards and intercept it. The driver would be surprised at first, then smile realizing that Peter getting ahead of him was meaningless. He would gun the engine daring Peter to either be run over or step aside. But Peter would jump at the last second locking his knees as he rammed his heels through the front windshield, probably breaking his legs and mortally wounding the kidnapper while the child sitting safely in the backseat would receive nothing more than a few bruises. Peter would then hem and haw over their small bruises while nobly ignoring the pain of his two broken femurs.

Now, sweating in the woods, he just wanted his kids to be safe. He didn't care if he proved anything in the process. If he could ensure his children's safety by sitting aside and serving lemonade while everyone else fought, he would do it gladly. It reminded him of what the old man had told him – something about succeeding by not needing to win.

But this didn't feel like winning. He knew he would do anything to keep them safe even if it meant having stains on his soul that didn't wipe away. Somewhere in the back of his consciousness, he knew that even if they all survived, the caste of their souls would be tested by the stains of what they had done to survive.

"What?" asked Peter being brought out of his thoughts.

"I said, did you hear that?" said Bryan, staring up at the path behind them snaking through the woods.

Peter tried to listen through, or perhaps around, the din of the Goblin horde below. He heard a noise like someone dragging something, then two thuds followed again by dragging sounds. After a minute, he heard loud snapping noises followed by heavy crashes.

"The dragging sound?" asked Peter.

"Yeah," said Bryan. "It doesn't sound too close. Do you want to go back and see what it is?"

Peter had two simultaneous responses vie for control of his brain. The I-need-closure-to-every-question side of him wanted to wander back up the hill. For one thing, they never got to see what came out of the cave. It could be a fuzzy Easter bunny for all they knew. And what was more interesting than unknown noises in a forest full of mythological creatures? It was another adventure of discovery.

However, the I-don't-want-to-die part of him was confused as to why they had stopped running in the first place. It didn't matter that they weren't being chased. They were *way* too close to whatever was coming, and he didn't want to become an example for the euphemism about curious cats.

But they needed to know what was coming. He knew the levee wasn't going to blow anytime soon, so it mattered.

"I think we have to see what it is. Let's go," he said starting back up the hill.

It seemed like a luxury to be able to walk up the hill rather than run. Two of the three Peters went wide to each side to provide better perspective in the event of an ambush. Bryan and the third Peter walked straight to the noise through the pine needle carpeted forest. Peter switched hands on his sword wiping sweat from the wire wound pummel on his cotton shirt. As they topped a rise, they saw it.

"What the heck is that?" asked Bryan.

"Ugh!" said Peter, "That's freakin' gross!"

The creature was still a few-hundred feet across a shallow valley, not very far from the crack in the earth. Peter estimated that it must have moved no more than one-hundred feet from the fissure in the time it had taken Bryan and him to run away, stop, hear the sound and then come back.

"At least it's slow," said Bryan, and Peter nodded. It was a darn good thing too.

It looked like a gigantic slug with six underdeveloped appendages crowded up on the first half of its body near the head. Peter was pretty sure it was the head for two reasons: he assumed it was moving headfirst like just about everything on this planet, and there was a suction cup looking hole where its mouth should be.

The mouth was horrifying. It was perpetually agape, allowing a perfect view of its hundreds of teeth spiraling throughout its five-foot circular opening. The tail of its body trailed off slightly into something that almost looked like a dolphin's tail but split off in two more blubbery appendages. The whole slobbery mess of a blob had to be at least twenty feet tall and fifty feet long if one was foolish enough to ascribe definite form to the thing. Its body was smooth and slimy but had rolling folds of fat, giving it a body-type somewhere between caterpillar and obese slug. He watched as the thing lunged forward, used its pudgy forearms to claw at the ground, and then pull the fleshy back half of itself forward. It couldn't have moved more than five feet at a time.

"This is going to take a while," said Peter.

Bryan sighed. "What is it?"

"Well, not a Dragon, that's for sure."

"How did that thing even kill the Dragon?" asked Bryan. "It looks like it can barely move."

"I'm more impressed that it beat the Ogre. The Ogre was ready," said Peter. "We should keep our distance."

"We should go back and help the others," said Bryan.

"Yeah, okay. I'll leave two of me here to keep an eye on it," said Peter. "I don't want it to surprise us by the stream in an hour or so."

When they turned their back to go down the hill, Peter saw through the others' eyes that the creature had picked up its head and was testing the air with its open, circular hole.

"It senses us," said Peter. "I don't know how, but it does."

They both crouched low getting ready for anything.

Bryan whispered, "What should we call it? It kind of looks like –"

Peter smiled, shaking his head. "Don't say it."

***

"Okay, texting didn't work, and calling didn't work. Any other ideas?" asked Erin.

"Yeah. Start the darn timer before you throw the phone in the tunnel," said Billy.

"I said I was sorry," said Peter.

They crouched behind a thick pine tree, Peter and Billy shoulder-to-shoulder peeking around the tree on either side, while the Ogre stood off to one side, unconcerned about any flying shrapnel. Peter wiggled his toes in his new running shoes, feeling the water seep out of his socks under the pressure of his toes. He hated wet socks. But he hated being the reason that the levee hadn't blown even more. He hated letting people down.

"We just need another way to ignite it," said Brad. "Ideas?"

Silence greeted the question.

"How much time do we have?" asked Erin. "How are the others doing?"

"Peter and Bryan went back to see what killed the Dragon. Fortunately, it's slow," answered Peter. "We should have some time."

"Like how much time?" asked Billy.

"Maybe an hour. It's kind of hard to describe," said Peter. "Bryan called it Turdzilla."

"Eeewwww," said Erin as Brad repeated the name a few times, testing the weight of it.

"Turdzilla," said Brad. "Alright, well I think I have an idea. We need to gather a few things, and if we have the time –"

"Wait!" said Peter, his red eyes staring into the distance. "What the heck? How is that possible?"

"What's possible?" Erin asked.

His eyes refocused and he turned to his three companions. "They're gone. All of them."

CHAPTER 25

Arthur had been the first one to drop out of the narrow tunnel. It ended like it began, as a thin crack in a wall of a larger cavern that led down to a flat surface at the bottom. They took their time crawling down to open ground, still shaken from the events of the cramped passageway.

After Caitlin's rainbow kitty had killed all the rats, they waited and allowed the kitten to heal most of their larger wounds. The kitten had spent the most time with Shannon who, although was now healed, needed more rest if her light breathing and drooping eyelids were any indication.

Arthur wasn't surprised that Shannon was tired. He had lost count of how many times, or for how long, she had used her stone. There was the house when the Ogres had attacked, in the woods when the log pile was on fire, and in the deeps when they had entered the narrow crack the old man mistook for a proper tunnel. Each time she used her stone, time moved more quickly for her, and after using her stone as much as she had, it would have felt like she'd been awake for almost two days. That would be tough on a normal day, but add being chased by monsters and nearly eaten alive to the menu, and that meant it was time for her to rest.

Arthur shivered as he remembered the rats. Like Shannon, he hadn't been able to fully turn onto his side to curl into a fetal position like Caitlin, but he hadn't been quite as wedged as Shannon either. At least in the beginning, he had been able to keep the rats away from his body by swinging his arms and legs as they attacked. His sight had been a huge advantage for avoiding most of the more painful bites, but it was a special type of torture being able to see each of the few-hundred rats biting him through his stone and not being able to do anything about it. It had been so much that he had considered dropping the stone and losing his sight. But that would mean not only losing his stone sight but also losing his regular sight and, even though they were in the dark, he was more terrified of not seeing than he was of seeing every detail of how he was being chewed to bits.

He had been scared and angry. Angry because Shannon and Caitlin were going through the same thing. He could see everything. He could see Shannon struggling to remain conscious. He felt his body convulse as he smashed his fists and legs up and down trying to kill as many as he could by crushing them against the tunnel floor and ceiling. But it didn't matter how many he killed, and he knew it. Yet smashing them made him feel better.

That was when he felt it. He felt his body growing. At first, his shoulders broadened slightly. His forearms became thicker. His fingers got thicker. He saw it happening with his sight and panicked. The anger was feeding his transformation into an Ogre.

If they had been in a wide-open chamber battling for their lives, he would have almost welcomed the transformation. The old man had said that it was inevitable, so he might as well put his infection to good use. But there, in the narrow cave, if he let his anger fuel the diseased transformation, he could grow too much and get wedged between the ceiling and floor. He could be trapped in the middle of the tunnel forever. He felt his chest growing closer to the ceiling of the tunnel and tried to calm himself. That was when the flash of light scared them off. Caitlin's rainbow kitty had saved them and might have possibly saved his life. Maybe all of their lives.

He had been the last one the kitty healed. He had watched with his sight as it healed Shannon, Caitlin and the old man. He would never have voiced it, but a part of him hoped that whatever magic allowed the kitten to heal their wounds would also somehow purge the Ogre disease from his blood. Even though his stone required no concentration to experience the wholeness of reality, he concentrated on himself hoping to see his body return back to where it had been, but it didn't happen. The kitten healed his wounds but did nothing for his deformation.

When they started moving again, it was much harder for him to move through the tunnel. His chest scraped against the cool, stone ceiling as he used the lubricating loose dust of the floor to aid his shuffling. His sight told him that he was now slightly bigger than Shannon was and much thicker in the shoulders, forearms and thighs. He used his sight to find the best routes, but it was slow going. He saw confusion and frustration of their slow pace turn to recognition on the old man's face. Neither commented on it, but Arthur knew the old man understood when he gave a short nod in the dark where no one would be able to see it other than him.

And now they were out in an open cavern sitting under the narrow tunnel. Arthur, Caitlin and the old man sat facing outwards in a triangle with Shannon sleeping in the middle. She had fallen asleep nearly instantly when Arthur had suggested it. Arthur could tell that the old man didn't like the idea of losing time for the rest, but he hadn't objected. He had, however insisted that Caitlin put her luminescent kitty into her backpack to keep them from being easily spotted. Caitlin hadn't been fond of the idea, but agreed. After a quick word with the kitten, it snuggled into her backpack and seemed content enough to settle down for a catnap.

Now that they stopped moving, Arthur was starting to feel the cold of the underground. He pulled his jacket out of the bag, thankful for having brought it. As he pushed his right arm into the blue green jacket, his forearm stuck halfway in. He forced it through, noticing the strain it put on the green thread of the seam. His left arm was easier, and he was able to get the zipper to his chin by blowing all of the air out of his lungs. Now that he had grown, the jacket felt more like a wet suit top. He was pretty sure that if he took a deep breath the jacket would split. The sleeves only covered two thirds of his forearms. Similarly, now the bottoms of his calves were showing from his too-short pants.

"How safe are we here?" he asked the old man.

"Relatively safe," replied the old man.

"Are we in the deeps yet?" Caitlin asked in a small voice.

"Yes," said the old man. "There are three levels of the deeps. We are now in the first and safest level."

"Tell us about them," requested Caitlin.

Arthur saw the old man reposition himself preparing his thoughts. "There are three levels to the deeps," started the old man.

"You just said that," said Caitlin.

"This is going to take a while if you keep interrupting," said the old man.

"And even longer if you say everything twice," answered Caitlin with such a twinkle in her eye Arthur would have sworn he heard a Tinkerbell ring to go with it.

The old man sighed and continued. "We are currently in the first and safest level." Caitlin coughed, but the old man continued unperturbed. "This level is called Extroc One. It holds the higher beings – both good and bad. Once I escaped my captor, this is where I was taught."

"Who caught you?" said Caitlin.

"It was the Whisp –" began Arthur.

"Do not speak his name here!" said the old man, looking side to side even though they were draped in darkness. "Names have power here. Do not call a thing by its name unless you want it brought into reality!"

"Okay," said Arthur.

"Who are the good people? Are they the ones who taught you?" asked Caitlin.

"Yes," said the old man. "In Extroc One there are two major civilizations that are generally benign and a few smaller groups that are not, like the Trow. The two major civilizations have very clearly defined territories and control most of what happens in this level. While they cannot completely contain the creatures of the lower levels, their presence on this level does help contain the deeper two levels. They guard their territory brutally."

"The Trow are a smaller group? I thought you said they fought in a great war with Ogres and had been around now for a thousand years," said Arthur.

"The Trow are a smaller group compared to the other two. Long ago the Trow would have been considered among the great civilizations, but over time their influence greatly diminished," explained the old man.

"What do the two civilizations look like?" asked Caitlin.

"They are called the Grith and the Elft. They are two very different peoples. The Elft are creatures that worship the wonder of life. They value beauty of art and intuition of the soul. Elfts are known to spend a lifetime perfecting how to commune with the unknowable. They are masters of the mystical arts," said the old man.

"What are the mystical arts?" asked Caitlin.

"Ah . . . that is a question best answered by the Elft. Though they would probably answer your question with more questions. 'What is the true nature of being? How do we know art? Is there any part of life that is not mystical?'" answered the old man. Arthur didn't need his stone to see the smile on his face.

"You spent time with them, didn't you?" asked Arthur.

"Just so," said the old man.

"What do they look like?" asked Caitlin.

"You will find out soon enough," said the old man.

"How?" asked Caitlin.

"We will need the help of both the Grith and the Elft to get to the next level of the deeps," the old man responded.

Arthur sensed them approaching as the old man continued. He wished the old man had described how the Grith and Elft looked. The ones approaching were small like the old man and carried sharp metal spears that were a little shorter than they were tall. Each wore armor made from dried chitin. He could tell it was chitin by the few minute pieces of insect flesh that had not been removed from the inner parts. Their faces were all sharp angles and taut skin with high cheekbones that stretched their skin like fiberglass poles holding up a nylon tent. Their bodies were similarly taut with dense, sinuous muscles. Each had fiery red hair down to their shoulders. They wore no shoes and padded in their direction in complete darkness. There were at least fifty of them.

Arthur whispered harshly interrupting whatever the old man had been saying. "A large group is coming."

The old man didn't look surprised as he stood up placing the heels of both hands on his back and stretching. "It is about time."

"Is it the Elft?" asked Caitlin.

"No," responded the old man, now facing the direction of the approaching group. "I present to you the Grith."

The old man grabbed a lantern out of Shannon's backpack and turned it on. The harsh white LED light revealed that they were surrounded. Caitlin mustn't have heard their approach because she let out a little yelp.

The Grith encompassed them in a half circle against the cavern wall. Most stood with their spears pointed at the ceiling in relaxed poses. Arthur held no illusions about their body language. It spoke to their confidence and assumed dominance, not to friendly intentions.

The old man called to the group, "As you can see a quarter of us have fallen asleep waiting for your arrival. Has the hospitality of the Grith fallen so that we are to waste away waiting for your escort? Who is your captain?"

The Grith closest to Arthur took a stiff step closer. "I am Captain Xyrth. Name yourself."

"I am known as Liam. We seek an audience with the Bone Lord."

"Liam!" screeched Caitlin, excited by the revelation.

Captain Xyrth flashed a smirk of annoyance. "You are mad, old one. We do not –"

"The guardians are lost, and the seal is near broken," he interrupted. "Creatures of the lower deeps walk the surface lands. Take us to Areon Kyll."

"You are not of the inner circle," sneered Xryth.

"We accept the gauntlet," said the old man.

Arthur felt tension rise in each Grith warrior as Xryth held the old man's gaze for a heartbeat. Whatever the old man was doing was making them uncomfortable and Arthur wouldn't have needed his stone to see it. Xryth waved his hand and all but three of the Grith left them.

The old man nodded to Shannon. Receiving the message, Arthur went to wake Shannon. After a good amount of prodding and subsequent grumbling, Shannon woke, and they were on their way. When Arthur started to untie the rope from Shannon's wrist, he noticed the old man shake his head, so he left them tied together. Xryth and another Grith wordlessly took the lead and the other two trailed behind the group. Arthur and the old man walked shoulder to shoulder with Caitlin and Shannon behind them. The stone path they tread upon had been worn smooth by many feet.

After a few minutes, Arthur was the first to break their silent trek. "Who is Areon Kyll and what is the inner circle?"

"Areon Kyll is the Emperor of the Grith. He is known as the Bone Lord. We will need his help to get into the lower deeps," responded the old man. "The Emperor doesn't grant an audience to any who request it. Only those in the inner circle can request an audience and the inner circle is limited to twenty of the smartest, strongest and most capable Grith in all the realm. They are his advisors."

"So how do *we* get to see the Emperor?" asked Arthur.

"By passing the gauntlet," said the old man. "An audience may only be gained by passing the gauntlet. That is what we must do."

"Do what? What do you have to do? Is it an obstacle course of some sort?" asked Shannon.

"To succeed in the gauntlet, we must defeat the inner circle in two challenges: one of knowledge and one of strength," said the old man.

"Is your name *really* Liam?" asked Caitlin.

"It is a name given to me by the Elft."

"Is it your name?" asked Caitlin again. Arthur could see that she was considering him with particular intensity.

"It is a name I have used," said the old man.

Caitlin held her lower lip between her teeth and tilted her head to one side considering his response. Apparently concluding something, she shook her head and waved away a thought with her right hand as if it were an annoying fly. She didn't believe him.

"How many people try to pass the gauntlet?" asked Shannon.

"Very few," said the old man. "Perhaps two or three each decade."

"*Decade!* I guess not too many people want to talk with the Bone Lord," said Shannon.

"What happens if we don't pass the gauntlet?" asked Caitlin.

There was a silent pause, followed by the clearing of his throat. "We will be cast into the lava pits."

CHAPTER 26

"Using the Grith calendar, the Ogre War started three days after the magnetic equinox in the year of 483 and concluded one-hundred-and-seventeen years later on the seventh day of the third month when the Torac House was defeated by the Slipth House," said Arthur with the rushed cadence and breathless word grouping that suggested uninspired recitation, the words themselves meaningless.

It made Caitlin think of the pledge of allegiance.

"Correct," said the old Grith sitting across from Arthur.

At least Caitlin thought the Grith was old. It didn't have a beard like Grandpa R. It didn't even have wrinkled skin, but there was something about the thin, grey-skinned creature that made her think he was old, very old. Somehow his skin held taut while giving the impression of sagging, like candle wax melting. Caitlin smiled at the idea of a candle. The fiery red hair topping its head even looked like the flame.

"Your question," said the old Grith.

"What is seventeen times nineteen?" asked Arthur.

Everyone groaned aloud. They had been doing so for some time now after each of Arthur's questions. Caitlin had lost count of how many questions they had asked each other, but it did feel like a long time. She was pretty sure she was going to need a bathroom break soon. Perhaps she wasn't the only one and that was why they groaned after each of Arthur's questions. This time the old Grith even bowed his head down and tapped his forehead on the thick onyx table a few times.

He answered without bringing up his head. "Three-hundred-and-twenty-three."

Shannon, sitting next to Arthur threw her hands up. "Buddy, you have to ask harder –"

"Silence!" said the Grith in purple robes at the far end of the table. "None may speak, save the two in combat."

Caitlin heard Shannon mutter something about the purple guy talking.

The old Grith took a melodramatic breath and asked his next question. "What are the seventeen tenets of the ancient masters?"

Arthur turned to the purple-robed Grith raising a finger. "Clarification?"

The Grith nodded in assent, then Arthur asked, "As described by Belorac or as in the new exemplification?"

The old Grith growled his response. "Belorac."

Caitlin wiggled her shoulder blades against her backpack as Arthur began reciting whatever it was that the Grith had asked. Judging by the Grith's reaction, he was answering correctly. Caitlin felt a small paw whap her in the left shoulder through her backpack's thin plastic lining. She giggled to herself and kicked her dangling feet.

That drew a sharp look from the old man sitting next to her. Apparently, she wasn't being serious enough. The old man had said that if they lost they would be thrown into lava pits. And when they had finally gotten here, he had gotten even more worried when Captain Xyrth said that the first battle was going to be against Kian. It was something about Kian being the most revered intellect in Grith history. The old man had been so worked up that Caitlin's stomach had started to feel tight. That was until she found out where they were having the battle.

She looked over and beyond Kian to what had to be the tallest bookshelves in the world – or under the world for that matter. The shelves looked like they were made of the same stuff that was on her kitchen counter. She thought it was called marble, but it didn't look anything like any marble she had ever seen. The shelves started at their level and rose up into the large vastness above their heads. She leaned back, tilting her chin up as far it would go trying to see the tops, but she couldn't. They disappeared into a grey darkness. They were taller than any tree she had ever seen. And they were surrounded by them. Each shelf extended out from this central table like spokes on the wheels of her *Hello Kitty* bike.

Each shelf held different things. Most held books, but she could also see tablets, scrolls and some random weird things that didn't seem to fit, like sticks with carvings or rope with a bunch of knots in it. And those were just the shelves that she could see. As she brought her gaze back down a thought struck her. What would happen if a book fell from the top shelf? If it hit someone, it would hurt a lot. And even if it didn't hit someone, it would probably smash to bits when it hit the hard floor. She imagined an earthquake. They would be buried in books!

But she figured it was a good thing they were surrounded by books. It meant that Arthur had full access to everything in them through his stone. Caitlin didn't know how his stone worked, but she did know that Arthur knew everything about everything within a half-mile of wherever he was. And if his answers to the questions were any indication, that included books. He didn't even need to open them to know what was in them!

". . . from now until eternity," completed Arthur.

Kian nodded, waving his hand in a dismissive gesture. "Correct."

Arthur looked at Shannon before asking his question. "What are the hit points of the Charizard EX in *Pokemon*?"

Kian turned to the purple robe at the end of the table. "Ruling please."

"Illegal question. The questions must be relevant to knowledge contained within the great library. Questions about your surface world are not relevant to this challenge. As we have discussed, there will be no questions about *Pokémon*, *Skylanders*, *Ninja Go*, *Dinotrucks*, *Cat in the Hat*, *Ninja Turtles*, *Mario Brothers* or *Star Wars*," answered the purple-robed Grith. "New question."

Caitlin figured it was a good thing that Arthur knew everything in the books surrounding them, but the problem was that Kian seemed to know everything in them too, even without the magical stone. Arthur had begun the competition asking about things from the books, but Kian knew them all by heart. So Arthur switched to asking math problems. They sounded hard to Caitlin, but the old Grith knew all of those too. So here they all sat, watching and waiting for a bathroom break.

"What is two-hundred-and-two times fifty-four?" asked Arthur who was then greeted with another chorus of groans. This time Caitlin joined in.

Caitlin rolled her shoulders and decided to distract herself from her bathroom needs by looking around some more. All twenty of the inner circle were sitting at the table. It was such a big table that all of them were sitting on the opposite side that she was on. They all were pretty much the same height. Perhaps that was a Grith thing, but they were not all the same width. Some of them were thin like Kian and some were thick around the shoulders and waist like a pregnant football player. She guessed that the pregnant football player types weren't there for their knowledge. The old man had said that they needed to beat the inner circle in a test of knowledge and a test of strength or else they would be thrown to the lava pits. She tried to pick out the one that would be picked for the test of strength, and she settled on the fattest one that also had the thickest arms. He looked pretty strong.

She felt her rainbow kitty shifting its weight in her backpack. The straps on her backpack were starting to feel heavy on her shoulders. She tried to remember what was in there but couldn't. The rainbow kitty was there, of course, and she was pretty sure there was food and probably a flashlight or two, but other than that she couldn't remember.

She looked over at Arthur. He was finishing another answer, and soon sour-faced Kian would say 'correct' and then Arthur would ask another question that was too easy. Really having to pee, on a whim she decided to whack Arthur with her backpack, hoping he'd get the drift.

Thwack!

"Owww!" said Arthur looking at Caitlin.

"Correct," answered the candle faced Grith.

Arthur rubbed his shoulder looking at Caitlin's backpack. Something sharp must have hit him, and though she had no idea what it was, Arthur would know what it was. Hopefully he also knew that her body was now at least eighty percent pee. She made wide eyes at him and, despite his eyes being closed, he furrowed his brows then smiled.

"I have a good one!" he said. "You're in trouble now."

Caitlin saw Kian roll his eyes.

"How many books are in the library?" asked Arthur.

The purple-robed Grith rose to his feet. "The number of books –"

"No, I will accept this question," said Kian waving at the purple robe. "Not only is that common knowledge among even the most neophyte scholars, but I'll have you know that I have spent the last few millennia as the solemn archivist of the great library. I have read every book within this library more times than you have read at all. I can read more than one-hundred books in a day and my memory is *pristine*." He stood and looked down at Arthur. "Surface dweller, you cannot win. I don't know how you know the answers to my questions but be assured I will find your ignorance and expose it."

Caitlin saw Arthur's smile fade a bit during the tirade.

"Could you please hurry up?" asked Arthur. "My sister here needs to use the bathroom."

Caitlin felt heat in her cheeks as she heard a few poorly suppressed chuckles.

The Grith scowled at Arthur and answered. "There are currently two-billion-four-hundred-and-sixty-three-million-nine-hundred-and-two-thousand-seven-hundred-and-three books in the collection."

Arthur turned to the purple-robed Grith. "Are we in the library?"

The Grith hesitated then answered. "Yes."

"So we are all in the library?" asked Arthur.

"Yes," he said again.

He unzipped the top of Caitlin's backpack and pulled out a hard-covered book about kittens who had lost their mittens and threw it on the table in front of the Kian.

"Incorrect. You missed one," he said.

The stunned silence was broken by Caitlin's small, giggly voice. "And Daddy told me not to bring that!"

CHAPTER 27

Caitlin was right about the fat one with the big arms. He was definitely the strongest.

He and Arthur were standing on opposite ends of a raised, circular rock platform. Caitlin figured it was about as big as their neighborhood tennis courts. The platform was raised to about eye level for Caitlin and it had no stairs or ladder, which meant that Arthur needed to take a big leap to get on top. The fat Grith, who was about as tall as Arthur, pulled himself up with his arms and then swung a leg over the top in a practiced motion.

After Kian had stormed off, they had been whisked away to the next venue for the strength challenge. Thankfully, the trip had been short, and bathrooms were near, if a bit differently arranged than bathrooms back home. The bathroom contained a hole in the floor and nothing more. It took a minute, but she made it work, and by the time she had gotten out of the bathroom, Arthur was chomping on a healthy spoonful of peanut butter and sipping from a water bottle as the old man talked to him about the challenge.

As far as Caitlin heard, there were three ways to win: knocking the opponent off the platform, knocking them out, or causing them to give up by calling out 'Father'. The old man warned Arthur against using too much of his Ogre strength. He explained that the Grith were very experienced with Ogres, and not in a good way. If they found out he was infected, they would throw him into the lava pits. Caitlin figured they could probably fight their way out if it came down to it, but the old man had said that they needed the Grith's help. So now Buddy was going to fight a big, fat Grith on a raised platform and, if he lost, they would all get thrown into the lava pits. If he won, but revealed his Ogre strength, they would get thrown into the lava pits.

Despite herself, with all the talk of lava pits, she was starting to get really interested in what the pits looked like. She imagined a *Mario Brothers* style pool of lava that they might practice jumping over. She wondered if fireballs came shooting out of the lava at regular predictable intervals like they did in the video game. Although if video games were going to help Arthur, it wasn't going to be *Mario Brothers*. This was more like *Smash Brothers*. After all, they were going to duke it out on a raised platform.

Arthur was given the choice of weapons. After discussing it with the old man, he chose a quarterstaff. Each competitor was given a rod of metal about as long as they were tall. When Caitlin asked why they were not made of wood, the old man explained that they don't have trees down here, but they do have plenty of metal. When Caitlin asked the old man what the books in the library were made of if they didn't have wood for paper, he told her that she didn't want to know. Instead of thinking about it, she decided to watch Arthur whip the shaft around his body in dizzying patterns. She guessed it wasn't too heavy for him.

A Grith in purple robes, this one different from the one in the library, called out, "the challenger and the incumbent will stand on opposite edges. Competition starts when both touch their staffs to the platform. Competition ends when either competitor touches the ground outside of the platform, submits by declaring 'Father', or is rendered unconscious or dead."

Caitlin whispered to the old man, "Are we allowed to talk in this one?"

The old man shook his head. Caitlin blew out a heavy breath and rolled her eyes at Shannon who rewarded her with a smirk. How was she supposed to help Buddy if she couldn't even talk?

Arthur and the fat Grith walked to the very edge of the platform and faced each other. The Grith was the first one to touch his staff to the hard marble surface. Arthur followed suit a second later.

The fat Grith rushed out from the edge claiming the center of the circle. Now that he had the middle, no matter where Arthur went he was going to be closer to the edge than his opponent. The fat Grith crouched in a wide-based stance that looked like a tree taking root. Caitlin looked over at Arthur who was still on the edge. He stood there in the same relaxed pose as when they had started. A minute passed, then two, and he continued to stand there some more. Caitlin smiled to herself.

He put his metal quarterstaff over his shoulders and looped both arms around in a relaxed T position. Apparently, Arthur wasn't too concerned with being near the edge and was inviting the weighty Grith to join him. The Grith looked confused for a minute, then started edging closer to Arthur in a wary crouch that assumed nothing.

He had seen what happened in the library, so the fat Grith was smart enough to not underestimate Arthur like Kian had. The fat Grith closed in on Arthur then lunged, jabbing with the base of his quarterstaff. Arthur reacted by twirling off the staff from his shoulders sweeping it around to block the jab, but the Grith had already pulled back on the feigned attack and spun around whipping the staff in a two-handed chop so quick that Caitlin swore she could see the metal bending on its way to Arthur's head.

Arthur moved quickly enough to bring his staff up to intercept the blow by locking both elbows out and accepting the blow in the body of his staff. Sparks flew as the mighty swing struck. A metallic squeal echoed through the chamber, causing

Caitlin to jump and cover her ears. She felt her rainbow kitty moving in her backpack. She looked up to see Arthur holding the two remaining pieces of his staff, one in each hand.

"Wait, wait, wait," said Arthur holding up a hand.

The fat Grith took a step back still holding a cautious crouch.

"I chose to compete with quarterstaffs. Mine is in half, so that means I don't have a quarterstaff anymore," said Arthur, facing the purple-robed Grith. "I get another one, right?"

"No," answered the Grith.

"Great," said Arthur turning to his voluminous opponent. "Then I should concede. I can't compete without a quarterstaff. How do I concede again?"

"You must say 'Father'," said the fat Grith.

"Ha!" said Arthur turning back to the purple robe. "He said it! I win!"

Caitlin let out a whoop and Shannon barked a laugh.

"No," said the purple one. "Continue!"

Arthur turned to his opponent and shrugged. "Oh well. I tried."

The fat Grith stepped forward into striking range. At least it was within *his* striking range. The Grith took a lazy swing, checking the distance, and Arthur deflected the swing. The fat Grith backed up and took another savage two-handed swing aimed at Arthur's center. Standing at the far edge of the platform, Arthur chose to duck and move around the blows rather than block them with his shorter halves. Occasionally he redirected the wide swings, sending high-pitched metallic snaps through the echoing chamber. This went on for a few minutes with neither combatant making any progress. Caitlin was starting to get bored.

"How can we help him?" Caitlin whispered to Shannon. "We aren't allowed to say anything out loud."

Shannon leaned down close to Caitlin's ear, pulling aside some of her hair to get close. "We don't have to say anything out loud. He can hear what we are saying right now. He has his stone and he can see our lips moving."

Arthur shouted above the sounds of the battle, "That's right!"

Caitlin looked up at Arthur then whispered to Shannon, "Was that for us?"

Arthur shouted again, "Yes, it was!"

"Was that one for –"

Shannon interrupted, "Yes. Yes, it was. So, we can tell him anything we want. But he seems to be doing fine."

They both watched as Arthur moved through and around the blows the fat Grith was raining down on him. Although none of the blows were touching him, Caitlin could see that he was starting to sweat, and he was breathing pretty heavily. It looked like a stalemate to Caitlin, just like in the library. Perhaps Arthur was setting him up for something.

As if on cue, Arthur ducked under the large Grith's quarterstaff and shot in close. The sharp metallic staccato of their weapons colliding was replaced with thick meaty thuds as Arthur used both halves of his quarter staff to rain a quick succession of blows across the Grith's body. He then leapt back as the Grith recovered from his wide swing. Arthur paused near the edge waiting to see the effect of his attack. Caitlin saw the Grith spit to the side and smile wickedly then begin to swing at Arthur again.

Something fell from the edge of the platform. Caitlin knelt down on the cool stone floor to pick it up. She rolled it between her thumb and pointer finger, feeling the smooth surface that ended in four sharp points. It was the Grith's tooth.

Caitlin held the tooth up to Shannon. "I don't think he is going to go down easily."

Shannon whispered back, "He doesn't need to. Arthur picked up a tree. He can pick up this guy and smash em'!"

"No, he can't. They know he shouldn't be that strong. If they see him do something like that, they will know he has the Ogre disease. The old man said they don't like Ogres here."

Shannon sighed and nodded.

"Ideas?" Buddy shouted.

"If he gets the Grith close enough to the edge he can just push him over. That doesn't take too much strength," said Shannon.

"Yeah," said Caitlin, then she whispered to no one in particular, "C'mon, Buddy. Get him close to the edge!"

Buddy dodged another blow and shouted, "How do I do that?"

"Oh," said Shannon. "Right. It looks like the Grith is too smart to get close to the edge."

"Yeah, I saw him at the library. He knows Budd is pretty tricky."

Caitlin saw Arthur smile at that one. She then watched as he cocked his head to the side, dodged a swing and darted in close, landing four blows on his way by. Again, the Grith seemed unfazed and turned to follow.

Caitlin knew he had a plan but couldn't figure out what it was. She hoped it would work. As interesting as they sounded, she didn't want to get thrown in the lava pits.

The fat Grith stuck to his same tactic and inched close enough to send in a flurry of heavy blows. This time instead of ducking under and weaving around the blows, Arthur used his two short rods to meet the blows head on. The impacts seemed to tear at Caitlin's ears and she covered them. Each time they hit, Arthur's feet skidded back an inch or two, and he was already near the edge and was inching closer and closer with each blow. Another hit sent half of his shoes over the edge.

"Buddy, watch out!" Caitlin yelled.

"Silence!" yelled the purple-robed referee.

The next strike sent his shoes right over the edge, and he fell off the platform, out of the crowd's sight.

"No!" shouted Caitlin and Shannon at the same time.

The old man cursed as the fat Grith bellowed a belly laugh and raised his hands to the crowd. Other than Caitlin, Shannon and the old man, they all remained silent. That seemed odd to Caitlin. Weren't they allowed to talk now?

The fat Grith smiled up at the purple robe on the raised chair, but he received no response. Caitlin was confused. Hadn't the purple-robed Grith in the library called victory? Why wasn't he doing it now?

She moved through the crowd, circling around the platform to see where Buddy fell. She saw the fat Grith moving to the edge to get a better look too, and they both saw him the same time.

There was Arthur, not touching the ground, but ducking low just under the ledge of the platform, his whole body pressed against the four-foot wall as he balanced on the end of one of his quarterstaff pieces like a stork standing on one foot.

The fat Grith stood on the edge, not sure what to make of what he was seeing. Arthur made use of his hesitation and jumped up. On his way up, Arthur placed the larger piece of his rod between the Grith's legs. Then, as he dropped, he pushed both legs down hard on the rod where it was hanging off the ledge, sending the other end hard into the Grith's crotch as he had seen in countless cartoons with seesaws and rakes. The lever-action picked up and threw the Grith over Arthur who had grabbed onto the edge of the platform making sure to not touch the ground.

The Grith fell with a heavy thud. The room was silent. Caitlin could hear Arthur's breathing from where she stood.

The purple-robed Grith stood on his chair. "Victory to the challenger!"

Caitlin was startled out of her stunned stillness when Shannon and the old man grabbed her on their way to Arthur.

"Come," said the old man, ignoring the yells of protest all around them. "We go to the Bone Lord. Now."

CHAPTER 28

Michelle, Judd and Jenn returned to the group, and it was clear that the battle was taking a toll. The group was near to the point of complete exhaustion and another attack might break them.

She didn't know how long they had been fighting, but by the way the group looked, they didn't have much longer. They were still surrounded, and they were getting tired. As she thought about it, she could see those around her starting to falter. She felt an icy tingling in her hand.

She mentally kicked herself. Instead, she concentrated on her admiration for how well the group had held together when she and Judd bolted off after Jenn. As she continued to fight, she mentally picked out each person in the group and considered their unique strengths; Marci with her axe throwing, Jenn with her tenacity, Judd with his mountainous size and strength and on and on. The stone warmed in her hand.

Without thinking about it, she started to shout her thoughts to the rest of the group, all of the cheesy encouraging things that she felt about each of them but never told them out of fear of seeming quaint or overly sentimental. Even now, with everyone fighting for their lives, she felt her cheeks redden as she threw off the insulating armor of rib-elbowing irony for naked genuineness. It almost felt as if she were a separate person hearing someone else talking. All of her protective filters were off. Somewhere inside she couldn't believe she was the one talking.

"Marci, you're my hero because you go to the gym and lift. I cannot believe how much stronger you have gotten since you started. Seriously, you have basically been swinging dumbbells for the last half hour and you don't even look tired.

"Jenn, I love that badass streak in you. The fact that you can do anything you want exudes from every pore in your body. You literally just pulled a fishhook from your thigh and then used it to take down some Goblins. How freaky is that?"

"Judd, you are a giant to normal people. These little things *cannot* be more than a slight inconvenience to you."

She thought she heard a snicker or two and she was sure that there had to be at least a few rolled eyes, but she had to do it. Her stone was white hot in her hand. The smell of burned flesh filled her nose as she continued to fend off the Goblins. She didn't care. She *had* to hold the bridge. Her children were down underground somewhere and no matter what needed to happen, she would do it. She squeezed the white-hot stone tighter and continued shouting her encouragement. Then everything changed. Their closed circle started moving.

They weren't just moving. After a few steps, they were charging. She didn't have much choice, and her years as a color guard in high school marching band gave clear direction - when in doubt stay between the two people on either side of you.

They charged into the Goblin horde, plowing over the first few surprised ranks before meeting any real resistance. Then, as the group clashed blades to blades, the combined momentum of the group caused the tight circle to rotate and slide around the resistance. Michelle felt the rotation happening and did her best to stay between Marci and the guy next to her. In doing so, the battle shifted from fighting the few Goblins in front of her to sliding across the battle line so that she was never fighting the same Goblin for more than one or two blows. The effect was devastating.

With the way the group was moving, they had taken the initiative of the battle and the Goblins didn't know how to react. Their spinning accelerated and it took a ruinous toll on the army full of evil little men. They cut through the mass, spinning like a weed-whacker through tall dry grass.

Now she was shouting. The stone was so hot now that she considered opening her hand, but instead she allowed it to burn. It was okay if it kept her babies safe. And almost as soon as it began, it stopped. Everything stopped.

There wasn't anyone left to fight. Their small group of a dozen had defeated more than an almost incalculable amount of Goblins. Her own ragged breath sounded like cannons in the fresh silence.

Movement drew her eye off near the stream where Bryan and the Peters had crossed. Two Peters stood dumbfounded, confused about what to do next. She forced herself to snap out of it and called out to the group.

Breathe. She needed to slow down her breathing.

Michelle placed her gaze on the ground a few feet in front of where she stood and focused her thoughts. She cleared her throat and called out.

"They are gone! All of them," she said, turning to look at each of them. "Fall back to the bridge, regroup and rest up. This was the warm up."

She flashed her best toothy wolfish grin and noticed a few others mirror her ardor. She held the grin until she worked the stone back into her left pocket. She felt a layer of skin separate from her palm as she forced it inside, the stone seemingly unwilling to break contact.

She looked at her hands. Both were covered with slick green Goblin blood. Her right still held the Trow sword she had collected, and her left hand had a stone-shaped burn mark that throbbed in sync with her heartbeat. The very center of the mark was charred to blackened gristle, which then transitioned to white dead skin surrounded by a ring of angry pink flesh. It reminded her of when she had accidentally kneeled on an extinguished, yet still very hot, metal sparkler hidden in the grass of her backyard when she was young. The mark on her hand held the same pinpoint burning sharpness that she remembered. Her throbbing knee also held that mark.

As the others started picking their way back to the bridge, she waited for the two Peters.

"How?" one of the Peters asked. "There were so many of them . . ."

"My stone. It works on other people just like it does for me. I think it gets hotter the more people I use it on." She held her left palm out and showed Peter the damage.

The air he sucked through his teeth made a soft sound. "Oooo, that doesn't look okay."

She waved her hand at him. "If you are concerned about this, then don't look at Jenn's leg. Oh, we should help with that! She needs to go back to the house."

Without another word, she turned and trotted off to help Jenn. She needed to get back to the house. The group decided to leave one of the two Peters at the bridge to help relay information through the power of his stone. The one Peter, Judd and Marci would be the backbone of the remaining group to guard the bridge, which now totaled about eight very tired and thirsty people. Michelle, a second Peter and a woman, whose name Michelle couldn't remember, were chosen to escort Jenn back to Billy's house. There they would grab some food and drink and then truck back to the bridge with supplies to feed the group.

"Oh, darn it," Michelle heard Peter say under his breath.

"What now?" asked Michelle.

"Billy and the others are still trying to blow up the levee," said Peter.

"Yeah, so?" said Michelle, trying to make sure she didn't trip and send Jenn sprawling to the earth.

"Well, they loaded the concrete tube up with propane and sealed it but haven't been able to light it to set off the explosion," said Peter.

"Yeah, I know. It was my idea," said Michelle.

"Well if they blow it up before we get back we won't be able to get back to Billy's house without either swimming across the hole they have blown in the levee or going all the way around the other way," said Peter.

Michelle grunted her acknowledgement. She hadn't thought about that. Billy, Erin, one of the Peters and an Ogre had broken off from the rest of the group to blow up the levee and were having trouble igniting it, which, as it turned out, might be a good thing. The trail that led to the woods was on top of the levee. It was the only way back to Billy's house other than going all the way around the lake which was at least two miles. They needed to cross before they blew it up. But that wasn't the worst part.

"You realize that if we cross before they blow it up we will be walking over a primed explosive that could go any second, right?" said Michelle.

"Not that this isn't a lot of fun," grunted Jenn through the pain. "But this *isn't* a lot of fun. I need to get somewhere to clean this out and sew it up. I'm pretty sure that fish hook wasn't sterilized in a certified autoclave."

"Okay, okay," said Peter. "I'll tell them to stop trying to blow it up, but we need to be fast. It's a sitting time bomb waiting to go off."

CHAPTER 29

"Wait! Stop!" said Peter said running up to Brad waving his hands. "Don't blow it up!"

"For crying out loud!" shouted Billy throwing his hand up in the air. "Why not?"

Billy, Erin and Peter were standing behind the cover of a tree a good fifty feet away from where Brad was crouched behind a makeshift bomb shelter. They had tried more than a few times to detonate the explosion with Billy's phone, but nothing worked.

Brad carefully set aside the wires. "What is it?"

"The Goblins are all gone," said Peter.

"Yeah, you told us that," said Billy coming to join them. "Somehow they killed all the Goblins. God knows how."

"I'm not sure I want to know how," said Erin, settling in beside Billy.

"Yeah. But Jenn is hurt badly and needs to get back to the house. Michelle and two others are carrying her back. If we blow the levee now, we are blowing up their way back. We need to wait for them to cross," said Peter.

"I wouldn't stand on that now," said Erin nodding to the primed and charged tube. "Even if it didn't explode while they were on it, if they are anywhere near it when it blows, they're going to get pelted with debris."

"I don't think it's ever gonna explode," said Billy under his breath.

"Actually, I'm pretty sure this will work," said Brad holding up the two wires.

It had taken some thought, but Brad had come up with an idea. While Billy and Erin stayed by the tube, Brad, Peter and the Ogre went to gather the necessary supplies: a long flag pole, electrical wire, duct tape (of course), a nine-volt battery and the electric starter from Billy's gas grill. With only a few Trow to deal with on the way, they returned to the tunnel and assembled their remote levee explosion starter under a backdrop of Billy asking why it was always his stuff that had to be mangled.

Brad ran the wire through the middle of the pole, securing the open ends on his side with duct tape. The other side was where the gas grill electric starter was attached in the tube about six inches in. Once it was together, they tried it a few times to make sure that the igniter sparked. To everyone's surprise, save Brad's, it did.

Then they bent the ignition end of the pole back on itself like a bendy straw to protect the igniter when the Ogre shoved the pole through the chunks of concrete and into the gas filled pocket. Brad was about to set it off when Peter had stopped them.

"Why don't you just send the Ogre to go get Jen? He could carry her with one hand and get her back to the house in less than a minute," said Billy, gesturing to the mountain of flesh and bone behind them. "She's probably used to being manhandled by Ogres anyway."

Erin's face scrunched up. "Billy! Is that a knock on Judd?"

"Have you *seen* how big that guy is?" joked Billy.

"Yeah. That's a good idea. Let's send the Ogre. Then we can blow it," said Peter.

Peter walked back to relay the message. The Ogre grunted a deep grumble in acknowledgment and trotted off up and onto the levee at a speed that would have been a sprint for anyone else. A heartbeat after the Ogre disappeared down the trail, Peter heard too familiar twanging sounds.

"Down!" he shouted. "Everyone down!"

An arrow whipped past his cheek before he had even finished yelling. He heard a scream of pain and looked to see an arrow buried in Brad's stomach.

"Gosh darn-it!" wheezed Brad. "That *hurts* like a —"

"Easy with the language, buddy," said Billy right before he levelled his rifle and took two shots into the forest. His bullets were returned by another volley of arrows. "They must have been waiting for the right time to attack." He kept his eyes on the forest looking for something to shoot at.

"Well the big guy is gone now," said Peter. "I guess they like their chances."

Erin knelt down next to Brad, "I'm trained in first aid. Do you give me permission to help you?"

"Yes!" said Brad. "Permission? Really?"

Peter didn't need to do anything to let his other selves know what was happening. It was happening to them through him just as much as it was happening to him. His twin walking with Jenn and Michelle knew. His twin with Bryan knew. His twin by the bridge knew and his twins making their way back to the bridge knew. And they all knew that there wasn't much they could do to help right now. He could just have all his twins drop what they were doing and converge on this point, but that was what got them into this mess, by dropping everything and sending the Ogre to help with Jenn. It was every bit as much likely that the Trow were waiting and watching the other groups for just the right time to strike too.

His stomach sank at the thought. He made a mental note to make sure that they never pulled too many good guys away from Billy's house, where the children were. He hoped Shannon, Arthur and Caitlin were doing better than he was.

Billy snapped him out of his thoughts by shoving a handgun into his chest. "Here. If they decide to charge us, shoot until it is empty. You're bound to hit something," he said with a wink.

Peter scanned the forest seeing nothing. Another volley of arrows came from at least twenty different places from the far side of the river. Billy took two quick shots right after the arrows were loosed then ducked behind the tree for cover. Erin had pulled Brad behind a grouping of three waist-thick pine trees.

"Do you have any allergies?" asked Erin.

"What?" asked Brad.

"When was the last time you ate today?" asked Erin.

"What does that matter?" Brad responded breathlessly.

"Can you tell me how this happened?" she asked.

"What? There is an arrow in my stomach! You saw it happen!"

Erin turned to Billy. "I think he is in shock." Billy grunted in response, not turning from the woods.

"I can confirm that. I am shocked," said Brad.

Another volley of arrows rained down and Billy took another shot.

"I think that was less arrows that time. You must have hit a few," said Peter.

"That or some of them are working their way around to come at us from behind," said Billy. "You said they can't cross running water. We should blow the levee now."

"Not yet," said Peter. "The Ogre just picked up Jenn. We need to wait for Michelle and the others to cross first. Then we can blow it."

"Ouch!" said Brad. "I take it back. I do not give you permission to help!"

"What?" asked Peter turning to look their way.

Erin looked exasperated, "He's in shock. I was trying to raise his feet."

"Here," said Peter, giving Erin the gun and moving back to Brad. "You're probably a better shot."

"No *probably* about it," Billy muttered through the side of his mouth.

***

Michelle rolled her shoulder, working the stiffness from it as she watched the Ogre running down the path leading to Billy's house with Jenn in arm. She was glad the Ogre showed up to carry Jenn. She was tired, and they had been making slow progress.

"We need to run," said Peter coming up behind her and the other woman. He put his hands on their back and unceremoniously pushed them forward at a trot.

"Why run?" asked Michelle, breaking into a trot.

"We need to blow the dam now. Billy and the others are getting shot at. Brad took an arrow in the stomach," said Peter still pushing them from behind.

"Umm, guys. What is that?" asked the woman helping carry Jenn.

Michelle looked up and saw something on the path. It looked like it had just stepped out of the tall grass on the hill leading up from the forest, for half its body was still hidden within the fescue. It was facing away from them, in the direction of the Ogre who must have just passed it. Its body was smooth and black.

It was low to the ground. Its muscular shoulders were no higher than her waist and its jet-black front legs came out of its body from the side like a newt rather than from underneath like a cat or dog. Only its front legs were visible, but that was enough. The thing flexed its long, hooked claws as it watched the Ogre. Even turned away from them as it was, she could see that its head was nearly twice as wide as its shoulders giving it a hammerhead shark kind of vibe.

Michelle put out both arms wide and stopped running.

"We need to –" started Peter.

She turned and slashed the air in front of him making a wide-eyed expression, trying to get him to shut up. She looked back to see if the black thing had heard. It was motionless, looking right at them, right at her, with its dead black eyes.

It took off after them in a full sprint, and if that wasn't enough, a trail of the black nightmares came crashing out of the tall grass behind it, soundless and keen on killing.

CHAPTER 30

"Now!" yelled Erin right before she ducked behind the pine tree.

There was a half-second pause when nothing happened as Billy held his cheek against the thickly-textured pine tree. Then he heard a surprisingly soft low whoomp sound. He had expected there to be a real explosion, like when they use dynamite in old westerns where dirt and dust is thrown all over the place in a firestorm of flame. Looking around he didn't even think it was any dustier. He held his gaze on the forest across from them, scanning for Trow.

"Well?" asked Billy.

"It exploded," said Erin somewhat noncommittally.

Billy took a quick look and Peter craned his neck to see.

There was now a depression in the path that Jenn and the Ogre had just run across. It was a few feet deep and ran the length of the levee right above where the tube ran. It looked like the tube just collapsed and the dirt above it had filled in. He could see water starting to work its way through the disturbed mass of dirt and stone, but it didn't look like it was going to do much else.

He looked back to see if anyone else was looking. Erin was chewing her lip with a worried expression on her face. Peter was kneeling next to Brad applying pressure to the arrow wound from both sides. Brad was laying on his side, facing away from the levee. The arrow had entered Brad's upper stomach at a downward angle and he could see the barbed tip just barely poking out of his lower back.

Billy looked again and there was a little more water bleeding through the disturbed layer, but it still wasn't enough to make much more than a large puddle at the base of the levee. A popping noise announced an arrow that lodged itself in the tree less than two inches from his face. He let out an involuntary bark and jumped back. He didn't fire back this time.

"How many left?" Erin asked.

"Bullets or bad guys?" asked Billy, not turning.

"Either," said Erin.

"I'm down to eight for the rifle and then I have a few magazines for the Glock," he nodded to the handgun he had given her. "After that it is a magazine or two between the Beretta and Ruger. Judd and I used a lot going door to door."

It sounded like a lot of ammunition, but it wasn't. Billy was the best shot, but handguns just weren't made for picking off Trow

238

from a distance. They would be ok if the Trow decided to charge them, but from what he had seen they were smarter than that. They were probably just hanging back trying to get Billy to waste his ammo. The fact that they hit Brad with an arrow was an unexpected bonus.

"We should leave," said Billy. "We set the thing off like we said we would. We should get back to the house before someone else gets an arrow."

He heard Peter ask Brad, "Do you think you can walk?"

Brad answered after a few labored breaths, "I think so. Definitely can't run."

"We can't leave if we are going to be walking. They would pick us apart as soon as we left the trees," said Billy. "Better to wait for the Ogre to return. He can carry Brad and we can run."

Another volley of arrows sprouted from the woods in perfect unison. The Trow were a good fifty to seventy-five yards into the woods, and that meant that the arrows shot out at a steep angle in order to reach them. Billy watched as the arrows peaked and then came streaming down at them. If the intention of skewering was removed from the whole situation, it would have been beautiful. As the arrows landed, he heard a clunk and a soft curse from Erin. She reached down and pulled an arrow from the tip of her sneaker.

"Small feet. Missed me," she said, winking at him.

Billy heard a trickling sound and saw that more water was bleeding through the imploded area. Some of the dirt fell off into a small pool that had formed at the base of the levee where the now demolished tube had once fed the stream. Billy took a few steps back, not taking his eyes from the forest, and handed Peter another one of his handguns.

"They might charge or they might have one of their annoying tricks," he said to Peter.

Billy checked that Erin had the safety off of the Glock in her right hand. He half-smiled to himself. She would have made a perfect hero if viewed from the elbow down. Her smooth white glove gave aesthetic contrast to the dark-black Glock 26 Gen 3. He looked back at Brad and Peter. Peter had put Billy's gun in the back of his pants and was helping Brad position himself before trying to stand up. Erin tapped Billy on the butt then went to see if she could help get Brad up without him needing to move too much.

Billy didn't have any doubt that he could get Erin back home. If they had to, they could take turns providing cover fire and leapfrogging back behind each other in a standard retreat, thank you very much History Channel. And if it came to it, he was pretty sure they could outrun the Trow to their house, which was less than a half-mile away. But Brad couldn't run. He would be impressed if he was able to walk at all. He would probably need help to walk on level ground, and they were at least twenty yards deep into the woods where he was going to need to step over, around and through brush and uneven terrain. It was going to be slow going.

Another volley of arrows forced him to step to one side. Luckily, Brad was behind a copse of trees and was free from all but the most perfectly- angled shots.

"I think they are getting closer," said Erin. "That last volley seemed closer."

Of course, they are getting closer.

He was surprised it had taken them this long. They had been shooting at them in regular intervals for a while now. From the multiple encounters he'd had the pleasure of enduring, Billy knew at least one thing about the Trow: they were almost never doing what you thought they were doing. Perhaps that was why he was almost relieved to hear that they were getting closer. It wasn't like them to hang back as long as they had. He was convinced that the Trow were firing on them to distract them from an ambush. In fact, the first thing he did after the initial volley was to look behind and to both sides for an ambush, but none came.

The familiar twang announcing another volley of arrows warned him enough to check overhead and adjust his positioning to make sure he was in the ballistic 'shadow' of one of the many pine trees. What must have been a disgruntled plant decided to reach out and scratch the back of his left calf as he adjusted his position. He turned to his left.

No more than twenty feet or so away was the darn levee that refused to submit to being destroyed. Small rivulets of water were still leaking through the displaced layer of dirt that had shifted down when the concrete tube had imploded after the propane tanks finally blew. What had happened was the equivalent of knocking out the bottom layer of a Jenga tower and, instead of falling, the darn thing happily fell upon itself and remained upright.

But that wasn't his main concern right now. What *were* the Trow doing?

They were pinning them down for some reason. And what was with the idea of firing in unison every minute or so? Why not just keep firing at random?

Just as another volley of arrows landed with their characteristic chorus of knocks and thuds, he became sure of their intentions. He crouched down to Erin and whispered harshly, "Erin! We need to leave. They are doing this to ambush us."

"No kidding. They are trying to pin us down. But I don't think they have tried to ambush yet because they don't have a good approach. Behind and either side aren't great approaches. We should wait for the Ogre to return, *then* we can make our way back to the house," said Erin, not taking her eyes off the forest.

"No! Think about it. What do we do every time they shoot?" he asked.

"Hide behind a tree," said Erin.

"Yeah. That and we all look up to make sure the arrows aren't going to hit us," said Billy.

"So?" said Erin.

"Why would they want us looking up?" asked Billy.

"I don't think they care where we look. They just want to shoot us," said Erin.

"Then why are they all shooting at the same time. All the arrows come at the same time, but it is easy to avoid them by standing behind a tree. If they came at random times, they would be harder to avoid!"

"What's your point?"

"Just go with me on this one," said Billy. "Don't look up during the next bunch of arrows. Keep your eyes down and right in front of us. I'll do the same."

Erin grunted which was her way of agreeing. Or perhaps it was best described as lack of disagreement.

Billy shifted back behind the tree closest to Erin and set his gaze in the middle distance just above the forest floor. The next explosion of wooden missiles streaked up and out of his vision. He grit his teeth, keeping his gaze focused down low, right in front of them and mentally crossed his fingers that he would be fortunate enough survive his choice to ignore the arrow's flight. The waist-high brush remained motionless, but he kept watching. The sound of the arrows breaking through the air became louder, warning of their descent. He bared down, gritting his teeth and kept his gaze down low. Then, a half beat before the arrows hit, he saw it.

At first it was movement from a single branch on a low bush perhaps thirty yards from the far side of the stream, then it became much more. The movement in the brush spread out in both directions parallel to the stream for at least twenty feet in each direction and moved four or five feet forward in one solid motion, then stopped right before the last arrow landed. His eyes widened, and he resisted the urge to shout. Whatever it was, was less than thirty yards from them. Erin let out a gasp.

"Shhhh," whispered Billy. "We can't let them know we know."

"It's sooo close," Erin squeaked.

"Apparently not close enough. But when it does get close enough they will spring it on us. We don't want to be here when that happens," said Billy. Then he turned back to Peter and Brad. "Get him up. We need to be ready to . . . Aww, what the hell?"

Brad was still in a lot of pain. His forehead and face were a little more sweaty than could be easily explained by the heat. He held his hands against the wound in his stomach. The corners of his eyes were creased with the force holding his eyes shut, and fresh blood had pooled under his back were the arrow protruded.

Why isn't Peter applying pressure? Then he saw him.

Peter was sprawled motionless, face-down next to Brad. The odd angles of his arms and legs suggested that he hadn't been conscious when he fell. Erin turned away from the stream to help them. She quickly looked him over as she crouched behind Brad and applied pressure to the wound on his back.

"What happened? Did he get an arrow?" Erin asked.

Brad shook his head in a small quick gesture. Billy could see that he was taking small, fast breaths now, and he was pretty sure that wasn't a good thing. He could see Peter's face, but he did look like he was breathing.

"Peter looks like he's been knocked out or fainted, and I don't think Brad is going to be walking anywhere," she said in a low tone to Billy.

Billy grit his teeth, then he held his hand back to her. "Gimme his gun. I only have eight shots left in the rifle."

She was able to get it without losing pressure on Brad's back. Billy shoved the gun into the back of his Levi Jeans and reset into a comfortable kneeling position scanning the woods the entire time.

"When they charge," he said in a low growl, "just keep shooting. No matter what, Erin. Don't. Stop. Shooting."

CHAPTER 31

The thick, palpable stench of the thing clung all around Peter and Bryan, so bad they could almost feel the slime on their tongues. Peter shook his head and snorted air out of his nose a few times in an effort to expunge the odor from his pallet. He was not successful.

"That thing smells as gross as it looks," said Bryan.

"I'm curious how it caught the Dragon smelling like that and moving so slowly," responded Peter waving this hand in front of his face.

Turdzilla, as Bryan had dubbed it, was now about half of the way to the bridge. They'd kept pace with it for the last half-hour or so as it methodically, if not gracefully, made its way towards the bridge using its sea lion-esque flopping to move itself forward. They hoped that it would wander aimlessly through the forest, but it had become apparent that it knew where it was going. It was making a straight beeline for the bridge.

Maintaining a safe distance, Bryan and Peter experimented with trying to coax it in a different direction, but nothing they did seemed to affect it in any way.

Peter felt Bryan looking at him. He knew he looked odd. It was probably his red eyes. Everyone seemed to either avoid looking at him or would hold his gaze too long as if to prove that they were unfazed.

"What?" asked Peter not turning to look at Bryan.

"What? What do you mean?" stammered Bryan.

"You stopped talking for a while there. You have an idea?" asked Peter turning to look at Bryan. Peter noted that Bryan concentrated on holding his gaze and not looking away.

"Where are the other two?" Bryan asked referring to the other two Peters that had gone out wide to either side of Turdzilla.

"They are keeping pace at about the same distance as we are, but off to each side. They aren't seeing anything different from what we are at the moment."

"How about the others?" asked Bryan.

"Oh! You don't know? Yeesh," said Peter throwing up his arms and mentally kicking himself. "Sorry, it's hard to keep track sometimes."

"Keep track of what?" asked Bryan.

"The Goblins are gone, all of them."

"Gone? Where did they go?" asked Bryan, confused.

"Um. They are toast. The crew down at the bridge went crazy or something, and took them all out," said Peter making non-specific gestures with his hands.

"Is everyone okay?" asked Bryan.

"Not really. Jenn got hurt and is being taken back to the house," said Peter. Then after looking a Bryan he quickly added, "Oh! Right. Marci is fine. Tired but fine. *Everyone* is tired."

Bryan heaved a sigh of relief. "How about the levee? Did they blow that up yet?"

"No. Not yet. They came up with another idea and are just setting it up now. They should try to blow it in a minute or two," said Peter, but that was being hopeful at best.

Peter checked in on their monstrous charge who was still chugging along. If Turdzilla got down to the rest of the group, it wasn't going to be good.

"We need to lead it away from the bridge," said Bryan.

"We tried that. It didn't follow. I'm not even sure it has eyes," said Peter.

"We *kind of* tried. We haven't gotten within fifty feet of the thing."

"What do you want to do?" asked Peter with a crooked smile. "Punch it in the chin?"

"Does it even have a chin?" Bryan smiled back. "No, we can't get that close, but we could try to mess with it a bit."

"Okay, I'm game. What's the plan?" asked Peter. "How do we harass a school bus-sized toothy slug without getting close?"

"I didn't get that far yet. I just know we need to keep it away from the bridge," said Bryan.

They both thought while watching the thing belly flop its way down the hill, crashing through waist-thick pine trees as if they were dry bamboo. Peter realized that getting closer would not only expose them to the risk of being eaten, but also being flattened inadvertently by the trees and general shrapnel thrown by the massive blob. If it could run through a tree without issue, they weren't going to be able to hit it hard enough to grab its attention. They needed a spear or something sharp that they could throw and get through its presumably rhino-thick slimy skin.

"Okay, you thinkin' what I'm thinkin'?" asked Bryan. Peter nodded and started stretching his arms. "A spear it is! Here, give me one of your swords."

Peter handed over the weapon. Bryan hefted the sword with one hand finding its center of gravity, then picked at its edge. It was well balanced, sharp and had a wire wound grip that was too small for his hand. He unlaced the leather string from one side of his armor.

"What are you doing?" asked Peter.

Bryan explained as he looked for a straight, reasonably-sized stick, "I'm making a spear. Well, more of a javelin. Perfect!" He kneeled next to the oak branch, hacked off a few of the secondary smaller branches, and then hefted it for weight.

"This should do."

He used the leather string from his armor to tie the sword onto the stick. The makeshift spear was about six feet long and twentyish pounds. Peter saw Bryan rolling his shoulder and frowning at the spear. Peter remembered that Bryan had messed up his shoulder a few weeks back at the gym.

"I'm not going to be able to throw this," he said, looking up a Peter. "My shoulder . . ."

"Yeah, no worries. It's not like I can miss the darn thing," Peter replied.

Bryan handed him the makeshift javelin. Peter tested it for weight, bouncing it in his hand before nodding to himself.

"I can probably throw this forty feet or so. I'll come at it from the side so that it is harder to miss. When it turns to follow me, I'll start off slowly at first. I don't want it to lose interest," said Peter, flashing a wink and a smile.

Peter jogged off into the woods where he could throw the javelin from the slug's flank. He and two of his twins positioned themselves to give a complete perspective of their target. There wasn't one inch of the slug that they couldn't see. Bryan had stayed back at a safe distance. Now in position, the Peter with the javelin waved to get his attention. Bryan waved back.

The javelin soared. It came out at an odd angle, almost thrown like a sidearm fastball rather than a high, arching throw from outfield to home base. Peter winced. It wasn't the throw he intended. With it thrown that low to the ground, he wasn't sure it was going to reach the beast before gravity took over.

As he watched its flight, it somehow continued to rise, peaking just before hitting its mark. The javelin struck the creature's side and sunk deeply. Turdzilla reacted immediately, curling up its massive body around the javelin working to get its mouth over the wound. Peter, who had retreated a few more paces, was jumping up and down letting out whooping calls to make sure that he got its attention. Turdzilla, oblivious to Peter's machinations, plucked out the spear and continued on its way.

Peter turned to Bryan and held his arms up wide, shrugging as if to say – 'now what?' Bryan returned the gesture. Peter waved again and held his sword up high then exaggerated an overhead throwing motion. Bryan shrugged back. Peter didn't think throwing another sword away was going to do anything different, but, then again, if at first you don't succeed...

Gunshots sounded off in the distance. Peter got a little closer this time and threw the sword just as he had pantomimed, holding it back over his head with two hands then whipping it forward to let it fly end over end. The rotating sword spun towards Turdzilla in a high arc like the one he had expected for the javelin. But the gigantic beast must have sensed it coming.

It turned to face the flying sword with its massive gaping circular maw. Peter thought it meant to catch the sword in its mouth, but when he looked back to see the damage done, something shiny whipped by his face at high speed, almost cutting his ear off.

A loud *thunk* drew Peter's attention to a tree twenty feet behind him. The thrown sword stood vibrating, buried halfway up to the hilt in a pine tree. As soon as his mind processed what had happened, Peter sprinted away from the monster, not bothering to look back. He shouted for Bryan to run, but he didn't seem to understand.

Peter could hear sounds of the thing convulsing. Then he felt it. His stomach lurched as he was lifted into the air and pulled back in the direction he had come. As his body accelerated towards the tooth ringed circle of death, he threw his arms and legs wide hoping to grab onto something. He felt his body rotate in mid-air, and turned to look just in time as a pine tree screamed towards him. His head struck it with a sickening crack, sending his body wide of its original path. His limp body hit the ground in a group of bushes not thirty feet from the beast.

***

Michelle didn't need to consult her fight or flight decision-making process. For one thing, Peter yelling "run" at the top of his lungs made his input pretty clear. They were also outnumbered at least two to one and it looked like a single hammer-headed over-sized newt would have given them a run for their money, let alone a pack of them.

Peter pulled at her shirt and pushed her in front of him. Michelle saw that he hadn't needed to do the same thing for the other woman with them. She was already halfway to the end of the trail where the levee melded into the neighborhood backyards on the far side of the lake. She must have started running as soon as she saw the things. Michelle wasn't sure if she admired her for being smart or was disappointed for being left behind.

A shockwave reverberated through her feet, accompanied by low *whoomp* as they ran to catch up.

Good. At least the levee is taken care of.

She imagined the water washing through the forest in a great wave, blasting back any remaining bad guys. She wasn't holding her stone, but the happy thought must have made her run faster. She couldn't feel Peter's hand on the small of her back pushing her along. That or he was getting slow, which didn't make sense. She was more banged up than he was.

She glanced back and saw Peter lying motionless face down on the trail surrounded by the pack of hammerhead newts. She whirled around, trying to understand what was going on. She didn't see any blood anywhere and from the way the newts were circling him, she didn't think they had caught him. Then one lunged forward, taking Peter's limp calf in its mouth, tearing at it like a dog working on a bone. Then the others started in.

CHAPTER 32

Another set of arrows impacted the trees and ground around them in a formless rhythm of beats. As they landed, Billy watched whatever was advancing on them take another few steps closer. It was a lot closer now, less than fifteen feet from the far side of the streambed. He figured one or two more volleys of arrows and then it would strike. They were running out of time.

He gave them a 50/50 chance of making it back to the house if they left Brad and Peter. Right now, that seemed like their best bet and he had to consider it.

No use in everyone dying.

He looked back at Brad. Erin was still holding the front and back of his torso, trying to use pressure to keep the blood in. Brad might not last the next ten minutes anyway. Peter was lying face down next to Brad and Erin. He looked dead enough.

But Erin said he was still breathing. For all Billy knew, he might have had a heart attack or something, or maybe that "magical" rock he had been carrying around had poisoned him somehow.

Still, Peter and Brad were mostly dead anyway, and only he and Erin would really know that they had left them alive. Well, mostly alive.

Erin wouldn't like it of course, but he could get through to her. They could either die here and now with these two or get back to the house and protect their children like they should have been doing from the beginning. It had made sense when they were trying to blow up the levee, but that didn't work. Staying here didn't accomplish anything except add his children to the list of orphans. It just wasn't right staying.

The problem was it wasn't right leaving either. He knew that. It didn't matter how you looked at it. It would be abandoning someone who was counting on him. His kids were back at the house and some of the neighborhood parents were watching them, along with some Ogres. He was counting on them to take care of his kids. Somehow, he knew they would never leave his kids, even if it meant getting hurt or worse. And he knew that he wouldn't leave these two even if it was a blockheaded thing to do. Erin's ringtone brought him out of his thoughts. It was a tinkly cell phone version of "Bippidty Boppidy Boo" from *Cinderella*.

"Oh!" said Erin reaching for her phone in her back pocket while maintaining pressure on Brad's back. "It's Catherine."

Billy grunted in reply.

"Hi. Yeah, no, it didn't blow. Well it did blow up, but the dirt just slumped over and is sitting there . . . Oh? . . . Okay, I'll ask." Erin's voice changed tone such that Billy knew she was talking to him. "Catherine has an idea how to break through the levee."

"Good. Tell her to do it ten minutes ago," answered Billy, as another barrage of arrows sailed overhead. It was only a matter of time now.

"But she would have to use your..."

Billy cut her off whispering harshly, "Whatever! That thing across the stream is inching its way closer to us and is going to break through the brush and be on us in *seconds*. Tell her to send help and do whatever she needs to do to break the levee, *now.*"

"Okay, okay," she said, flashing him a look. "Catherine, do it fast and send help. We don't have much time."

"Billy!" called Erin after hanging up. "Peter's bleeding!"

Billy took a quick look, then did a double take. Peter wasn't bleeding. He was spouting blood like a punctured waterbed. Not only that, but Billy swore that he saw a gash appear out of nowhere on Peter's right arm. Billy slung his rifle around his shoulder and crawled back.

"What's going on?" asked Erin, panicking. "He's just bleeding for no reason."

A deep gash materialized on Peter's leg, the skin splitting and filling with blood as Billy watched.

"It's that damn stone," said Billy reaching for Peter's hands. "It's doing something to him. They said they were dangerous."

"Don't touch it!" warned Erin.

Billy pried open Peter's left hand, but it was empty. He reached over to pry open his right and a medium-sized red stone fell out of his palm into the leaves and dirt of the riverbank. Billy held his breath watching. Peter's arms and legs stopped producing wounds.

"Okay, I think that did it," Billy said, letting out a deep sigh. He took off his shirt to tourniquet some of the larger wounds. In the background, he heard a high-rev engine coming from the lake.

"Wait a minute," he said, slowly raising his gaze to meet Erin's. "What did Catherine want to do?"

"You said it was okay . . ."

"Please don't tell me that she —"

Billy was cut off by the sound of thrashing leaves. He turned to see dozens upon dozens of dark-black, panther-sized, salamander-looking nightmares breaking through the brush on the far side of the stream. They were coming right at them. He levelled his rifle, hands shaking.

The engine tone peaked and became louder. It wasn't until he had heard the second or third shot that he realized he was firing his rifle into the oncoming stampede. A second pattern of shots told him that Erin was doing the same. There were too many coming to hope to survive, but there would be a heavy toll to pay. That he and Erin would guarantee.

***

The sword in her hand rubbed painfully against her burnt palm as she raced back to where Peter had fallen. He was surrounded by seven of the midnight-black beasts.

She tried to work her hand into her pocket as she ran to Peter, but she didn't dare slow down to make sure she got it. She arrived at the pack without her stone in hand and swung her Trow sword hard at the nearest black hammerhead newt. Dark ichor spouted as the thing collapsed under her blow, giving her a clear view of Peter.

At least it would have had he been there.

He was gone.

Her mind struggled furiously. He had *just* been there. They had only been on him for a couple seconds. Somewhere in the back recess of her mind, she noted that if Peter had been consumed that quickly there would have been much more gore on the dirt path.

Still confused, she inspected the path. Small pools of dark wetness stained the red clay dirt and exposed rocks of the path, but definitely not enough to suggest that the newts had completely consumed him in a matter of seconds. But he couldn't have slipped away either. He had been surrounded.

Michelle's mind was still working away when she realized that six pairs of dead black eyes were looking right at her with insect-like stillness. She knew that stillness belied what was to come. As soon as whatever primal sense they had was done evaluating the situation, they would be on her like a school of piranha, just as they had done to Peter. As close as she was to them, she didn't dare back up. That would be a clear sign that she was prey. Her grip on the Trow sword tightened as she held her ground.

All seven heads turned to the lake when a high-pitched motor sound pierced the air. She could feel the weight of their gazes being lifted off her as they turned.

Soft steps.

Slowly backwards.

The motor got louder, and she saw a speedboat come around the far side of the lake, which didn't make sense for a number of reasons. First, their lake didn't allow motor boats of any kind, so no one kept them on the lake. Second, the lake was large, but relatively narrow and convoluted. It wouldn't have been out of the question for someone to mistake it for a wide, still river, and that meant that speedboats wouldn't have the room necessary to turn at any speed above a slow crawl. Whoever was driving this boat didn't seem to understand that fact, and was moving at what would literally be breakneck speed. The front half of the boat was kicking up out of the water as it streaked across the lake right at the levee. It looked like it was gaining speed.

She took another step back and then another.

Distance.

She needed distance between them and her while their attention was drawn elsewhere. She could have reached out to touch the nearest black hammerhead.

The heel of her foot landed half on a fist-sized stone causing her to stumble to one side. The pack turned in unison as if she had clapped her hands for their attention. She brought her sword out in front of her body. If there was going to be a feeding frenzy, their first taste would be iron.

The sharp snapping of fiberglass and the screaming of tortured metal filled the air as the boat crashed against the levee. Dirt, water and boat pieces were thrown high into the air like fireworks that had been set off too low to the ground. Even though it was more than two-hundred feet away, Michelle and her dark friends were treated with a gentle misting of dirt and water. Then she heard the most wonderful sound, the sound of water flooding down through the breach in the levee.

The formerly placid lake became choppy, presented with a new path to flow. Large unstable whirlpools lived out short lifetimes as they coalesced, amalgamated and faded each second as massive volumes of water left the lake. Muddy shoreline began to appear around the lake like a coffee stain. On the forest side of the levee, she could see treetops sway as the churning water cut through the previously dry streambed and overflowed onto each bank. There was no way a dam was going to survive that. A giddiness welled up within her. It was all she could do to not let out a whoop of victory.

Then her air was gone. She was on her back with heaviness pressing on her chest. She tried to bring her sword up to slash, but it wouldn't move. She felt sharp pressure on her forearm followed by excruciating pulls. Something latched on to her right thigh, then her left leg and the side of her stomach. She struggled to keep her breath.

There were too many of them. Everything was frantic movement and pain. She couldn't make sense of it. It was getting darker. They were blotting out the sun. She couldn't seem to draw a breath, and the weight on her chest was suffocating. They were all on her at the same time. Her strength was leaving, her arm muscles yielding to the wrenching tugs.

Then the pressure was gone. Air rushed into her lungs. She pulled it in with everything she had, gasping for it.

They were on her and then they weren't. She squinted up into the sunlight trying to understand what happened. A large form blocked the sun. She turned to see a massively wide body standing over her, thick meaty hands stained black with dark ichor. The Ogre smiled lopsidedly at her, if such a thing was possible from its malformed face. She took a few more ragged breaths before speaking.

"Where did you come from?"

The Ogre glanced back at the rapidly emptying lake. Deep Ogre-sized footprints led up through the muddy shoreline. She looked more closely at his soaked, misshapen body and recognized some of the patterns of scars.

"Weren't you supposed to be helping the kids get to the cave?"

He shrugged noncommittally.

For half a second, she was so happy to be able to breathe that she wanted to hug the big oaf. She groaned as she sat up. "Damn, you guys come in handy. I'm glad you're on our side. Help me up, will you?"

CHAPTER 33

The rushing water whipped Peter's limp body side to side. Billy's one arm gripped a pine tree and the other was wrapped around Peter's chest. The textured bark provided extra grip, helping him from being taken by the rapids and, at the same time, introduced him to a new level of brush burns. Billy was doing his best to keep Peter's head above the water but being waist deep in the raging water and holding him up with one arm wasn't helping things.

Erin had reacted quickly and dragged Brad farther up the bank of the stream. Billy hadn't been so fast. Not that he had any warning of what was going to happen. Erin had known. She had known that Catherine was going to kamikaze *his* speedboat into the weakened levee. Why was it always his stuff that got wrecked?

His cell phone, his boat, his house. All he knew was that someone was getting a bill for all of this and it wasn't going to be him.

"Billy!" he heard Erin shout. "Hold on! Help is coming! I can see them."

He wasn't sure he needed more *'help'*. They would probably come up with a plan that required crashing his extended-cab special edition silver F-150 into a telephone poll.

To be fair, the weird, black lizard things that were about to eat them were gone. There had been enough time for Billy to pick off a few when the water swept through, but it hadn't washed them away. It blasted them away like a bomb exploding. The few that had been in the direct path of the water vaporized, throwing a fine mist of black blood that might as well have been ink for the way it stuck to Billy's cloths. The rest had been thrown violently back into the woods where the trees played plinko with their bodies. He would be very surprised if any had survived.

That, of course, explained why the Trow had chosen to stay back and fire arrows from a distance. They had remained far back from the stream the entire time, and probably hadn't experienced anything more than a stiff breeze when the water rushed into the streambed.

"Hold on! We're coming," said a voice he remembered.

Billy turned to see a thoroughly-soaked woman with black hair come wading through the water. Other than being wet, she seemed unharmed.

"Well you seem perfectly unscathed," spat Billy out of the side of this mouth.

Catherine took Peter's legs and lifted them out of the water. Billy relaxed his grip on the tree and straightened up to better support his half of the weight.

"If it is any consolation, I skinned my knee real bad," said Catherine flashing her best mischievous smile. "I jumped out a half-second late."

They made their way out of the water and into the nearest backyard. The way was surprisingly treacherous. Either the Trow had lost interest or they had been warded off by the moving water because no more arrows were sent in their direction. They had to stop more than a few times to untangle themselves from underwater brush hidden by the muddy water.

"If I didn't know any better, I might think you enjoyed destroying my boat," said Billy as they placed Peter down onto the manicured lawn.

"Well it is a good thing you know better," said Catherine, still smiling. Then she frowned and looked around. "Where's Brad?"

Billy pointed with his chin to where Erin had pulled Brad. There was an ugly red trail through the grass leading up to where Erin was trying to hold close his wound. Catherine scrambled over to him and did what she could to help. A group of three arrived from the house with plenty of guns, but one too few makeshift stretchers. They decided to put Brad on the stretcher and carry

Peter. They said it was because they needed to keep Brad from moving due to the arrow, but Billy figured it was more because, as the conscious of the two, Brad would be more vocal about being jostled.

As the others started off, Billy doffed his cap and looked back to the scene of his boat's honorable demise before joining the procession back to his house.

CHAPTER 34

Shannon stumbled on the uneven steps as they made their way up the narrow, spiraling stone staircase. She wasn't counting, but it had to be the fifth or sixth time she caught herself on their way up. Light was non-existent but for a weird green luminescence that came from nowhere and everywhere, and it was only strong enough to give the faintest outline of the stairs and the rest of the group.

Arthur was in the lead, followed by Shannon, Caitlin and then the old man. In front of Arthur were the two purple-robed Griths that had judged the competition, and in front of them were the two Griths that had battled and lost to Arthur. Shannon was pretty sure she had heard their names, but, as it often happened, she forgot them almost as soon as they were said. Sometimes catching and retaining names was like trying to catch a ball that had been thrown five minutes ago. By the time she realized that she should try to remember a name it had already been said and lost.

Of course, Arthur was having no problem with the stairs. He didn't even have his eyes open. She probably wouldn't do any worse with her eyes closed. She could hear Caitlin falling all over herself just like she was. But that was it. None of the Griths nor the old man were having trouble. She knocked her shin on a step that was twice as high as the rest.

"Ouch!" she called out rubbing her leg. "What is wrong with these steps? They are all uneven. Can't they build a staircase with better stairs?"

None of the Grith acknowledged the comment, but she heard the old man from behind. "The Grith are a warrior civilization. The Bone Lord is their warlord. This is their stronghold."

"What does that have to do with building junky stairs?" asked Shannon. "You would think a palace would have decent stairs."

"Not a palace. A stronghold," answered the old man. "Have you noticed that the Grith move quite well over the same stairs that trouble you?"

"Yeah. They have probably climbed this staircase a hundred times."

"Exactly."

"Exactly what?"

"You are an outsider. Imagine an attack that made it to this staircase. The unevenness of the stairs would make fighting difficult for the outsiders but trivial for those who are defending, since they've climbed these stairs a hundred times and know where the odd steps are," said the old man. "Everything here is designed for utility."

"I don't think funny stairs are going to hold off an attack of Trow," said Shannon, starting up the stairs again.

"No, it wouldn't, not by itself. Notice how the staircase winds up clockwise and how narrow it is?" said the old man.

"So?"

"Those coming up the stairs would have to attack by swinging from left to right, which is awkward for a right-handed fighter. The defenders would have the high ground and would be able to swing right to left using the curve of the stair well to their advantage. The narrowness of the stairwell means the challengers must attack one at a time. A well-trained Fist of Grith could hold this stairwell against hundreds of Trow," said the old man.

"An Ogre would just blast through them," said Shannon, stubbing her toe on yet another step.

She heard the old man sighed before commenting. Perhaps she shouldn't have reminded the Grith about Ogres since they were trying to keep them from finding out about Arthur. Apparently, they didn't like Ogres.

"This stronghold has been attacked many times and no force has ever made it to these steps. The stronghold was built underneath pools of lava. Tunnels and stairwells can be flooded at will. Not even an Ogre could withstand that," said the old man.

Shannon thought about hot air rushing down the stairs ahead of a wave of red-hot lava. She looked up at the dark outlines of the Grith preceding them. She wasn't sure if she should be impressed or disgusted.

On second thought, the Trow had nearly brought her house down on her family just this morning. She figured that if she lived anywhere near the Trow, her house would need to be just as functional.

Her heart skipped a beat when she saw a red glow coming from the top of the stairs. A wall of heat hit her face as she took the last step. Then the stairs ended into a large cavern with two lake-sized pools of lava that provided the only illumination that the cavern needed. Unlike the rest of the stronghold, the floors and walls were smooth as glass. The far end of the hall held a raised golden throne with ten simple chairs on either side forming a half circle. Shannon could see that the throne was occupied as well as all but two of the chairs. She figured the two chairs were for the two Grith Arthur had challenged. The party continued walking toward the dais.

Arthur whispered to the old man, "So, what's the plan?"

Shannon could barely hear his reply. "I will do the talking. We will ask for the Bone Lord's help entering the second level of the deeps."

Shannon whispered, "Why do we need his help?"

"One does not simply walk into the second level of the deeps. It would be like diving into a pool filled with sharks. We need a significant diversion."

Shannon smiled. "Loooove it. The old throw-a-rock diversion." She didn't need to see Buddy to know that he was rolling his eyes.

"Yes, something like that. If the Grith can press an attack to draw attention, we may be able to slip in and avoid notice."

The four Grith in front stopped walking and kneeled. Shannon heard the old man hiss something about getting down. She looked behind to see the rest of them on one knee and realized that she was the only one standing. She shrugged and kneeled like the rest. They stayed like that for a solid minute.

The Bone Lord's voice sounded like rolling thunder. "Kian and Sojo. What say you?"

They both answered in unison, "We have failed you my lord. Our lives are forfeit."

The Bone Lord spat. "To the pits with them!"

Shannon heard Caitlin gasp. Arthur turned back to the old man and whispered harshly, "What is this?"

The old man did not raise his gaze and spoke his answer into the floor. "Turn back around! We are not permitted to speak yet."

Kian and Sojo were led by the purple-robed Grith back to the lava pools.

Shannon could hear Caitlin starting to cry. "No . . ." she said softly between sobs.

Shannon looked back at the two Grith who were about to die because Arthur beat them. Because they needed help to save their families. Why did they have to die? It didn't make sense. She was a good guy and so were the Grith. Why would anyone have to die? She was still tired from using her stone and crawling through the "tunnel" on her back. She had nearly been eaten alive by rats and now they were supposed to kneel here while two of the good guys died. It wasn't right!

She stood up. "Stop!"

Several things happened all at the same time. Kian and Sojo's procession to the lava pits stopped. That was a good thing. But she also heard the old man growl to himself. She figured that was a bad thing. That and all the Grith who had been sitting in a semi-circle were now standing. Standing with menace in their eyes.

She hadn't really thought of what to do next, but she had to say something. "We are all fighting the same thing. Why would we kill two of our own? We would only be helping the enemy."

The Bone Lord's voice rumbled where he sat on his throne, "Kill them all on my command."

The old man jumped up behind her, "My lord, please forgive us. These three are from the surface world. They do not know what they do. We have traveled from the surface to your great stronghold and passed the gauntlet and ask your favor."

The old man paused and took a step back. The entire room held frozen waiting for the Bone Lord's response. None came. Shannon figured the old man took that to mean the Bone Lord had decided at least for now to listen. She noted, however, that he had not rescinded his command to kill on his mark nor had the eighteen of the inner circle sat back down.

"We have passed the gauntlet and are now before you to join the inner circle," said the old man.

Shannon took a step back as it hit her. Now it made sense. The old man had said it before. Only the inner circle can talk to the Bone Lord, and they needed to talk with the Bone Lord to ask for help. They had to pass the gauntlet to talk with him. There were only twenty in the inner circle. When Arthur had defeated Kian and Sojo it had been a death sentence for them. The old man knew this.

Shannon turned to the old man. "You knew this would happen. Didn't you?"

Caitlin was still crying on the floor. Arthur was now standing, holding his position between the eighteen Grith of the inner circle and the rest of his group.

The old man ignored Shannon. "As is customary for a new member of the inner circle, we ask of you one request."

"I won," said Arthur, facing the throne. "The request is mine."

"Yes. Go ahead," said the old man.

"Buddy . . ." started Shannon.

"I request that Kian and Sojo be spared," said Arthur.

"No!" hissed the old man from behind Shannon.

"Your request is denied," rumbled the Bone Lord.

"What?" asked Arthur. "I won! That is my request."

"My lord . . ." started the old man again.

The Bone Lord's voice struck through the hall like thunder. "Silence!" The quiet seemed to throb for a brief moment before the Bone Lord continued. "What you ask is blasphemy. What you ask would be the end of the Grith! The strength of our people is what has allowed us to thrive for a hundred millennia, what has defeated the Trow in the Ogre wars, what will continue our civilization for eons to come. It is a strength born of the primary law of existence, the only law. The weak shall perish and the strong shall thrive. Weakness is a disease to be purged." He stood and gestured to the eighteen of the inner circle. "The inner circle is no different. Those two have been defeated. They must perish."

Shannon looked wide-eyed back at the old man, who shook his head miming 'no'. She didn't care. It wasn't fair. It didn't make sense. How were they supposed to make the world right by hurting the people who were willing to help?

"You aren't making any sense!" shouted Shannon. "Those two could help. They may have lost, but that doesn't mean they can't help!"

276

"Enough," said the Bone Lord with a low intensity that projected more rage than greater volume could have done. "Poison mixed with wine can only be poison no matter the amount. A diseased finger can be severed or left to fester and infect the rest of the body. Weakness forgiven is frailty encouraged. Any who further raise this question will be thrown in the pools with them."

The Bone Lord waved to the purple-robed Grith who had stopped the procession. Shannon saw them nod and continue walking with Kian and Sojo in tow. How could they just walk to their death like that? Didn't they want to live? She looked back at the old man. He was still down on one knee. He didn't look at her this time. She walked over to Caitlin and knelt beside her. She tensed when she heard Arthur speak.

"My Lord, I wish to change my request," said Arthur with a full voice.

CHAPTER 35

Arthur stood between the Bone Lord and the rest of their group. He was careful to maintain a relaxed stance despite the tension building in his body. They were standing in front of the equivalent of a rabid dog and to show weakness would be an open and clear invitation to attack. He wouldn't have needed his stone to see the aggression and dominance in the Bone Lord, but he did have his stone and it told him so much more.

He remembered very little of the information he had absorbed in the library. Apparently, he didn't have perfect retention of what he saw with his stone, but he remembered enough to know that the Grith before him was powerful, dangerous and, above all else, *evil*.

As soon as they had walked into the library, he knew everything. Just as the stone had allowed him to experience every last detail of the forest, it had shown him everything contained in each of the millions of books. All of the histories, philosophies, sciences, mysticisms, and theologies had become a part of his awareness. It had allowed him to defeat Kian, but it had also shown him the sum total of the Grith recorded consciousness. It was like remembering a book he had read a year ago. He couldn't recite passages, but he did retain the general story.

Long before the different levels of the deeps existed, a tribe of creatures carved out a habitable zone separate from the wilds. Over time, the prosperous tribe grew and expanded into what was now called Extroc One. Over hundreds of thousands of years, the great civilizations of Extroc One developed from that tribe: the Grith, Elft, Trow and others. For the next hundred-thousand years, the civilizations vied for power and territory, often waging massive wars. With the conclusion of the last of the Ogre wars a few millennia ago, Trow dominance was quenched and the Grith rose to supremacy. The general leading the Grith army to victory was Areon Kyll, the Bone Lord.

His exploits were legendary among the Grith. During a military transport, the entire north-western division had been ambushed by over a thousand Ogre Death Squads. As a newly-minted sergeant, his detail had been the only to survive, though how they managed to survive was never recorded. Later as a major general, he was the first Grith in over one-hundred-thousand years to attack a civilian target, forcing the Trow to either abandon their raids on the Grith army or abandon their loved ones. As expected, the Trow retreated right into a waiting ambush set by Areon.

The results were devastating for the Trow and the battle has been considered by many to be the turning point of the war. In that one campaign, Areon had sealed himself in the annals of Grith history, giving birth to what he described as absolute combat, where the only thing that mattered was defeating your enemy. Over the course of the next ten years, the Grith army under his control decimated the Trow opposition, which was impossibly fast compared to the standard wars which had been measured in centuries, not decades.

However, victory had not quenched his fiery heart. As warlord, he brought the concept of absolute combat to bear at home. The rule of law was replaced with the rule of might. Every civil conflict was settled by duels, preferably to the death. Advancement and mating rights were given to those who showed the most aggression and power. Social class was replaced with war class with the highest rank being the inner circle. All were subject to what Areon called 'the universal rule of power' and could be challenged and supplanted. True to his rule of power, all were free to challenge him in combat for the right to rule, and for the first hundred years, many tried, though none succeeded. Each time he dispatched his challenger, he took their left thumb bone and bound it to his chitin armor as a trophy. The Bone Lord had been born.

Arthur knew there were eight-hundred-and-thirty-two thumb bones on the Bone Lord's armor. The pale yellow and white bones ran in vertical rows all along the front and back, two levels deep. His reputation preceded him and had been greatly detailed in many books in the library. In the thousand years that he had ruled, none who challenged the Bone Lord ever survived.

But the Bone Lord was wrong. He *was* evil. He was part of what they were fighting. Organized intimidation and aggression was still aggression. Being mauled by a wolf-mole thing was no different from being killed in a ritualized duel. It might have looked a lot more organized, but it was the same thing. The Grith had wanted to save themselves from being overtaken by the wilds of the deeps, but it had grown and festered among their ranks without them even knowing it. The Bone Lord had to be stopped.

Arthur knew he couldn't do anything. He saw everything in the library. The Bone Lord was inhuman. He was unbeatable. Nothing could be done. It wasn't his fault, but his heart couldn't accept it. There had to be something.

Even though there was no need to do so, Arthur concentrated with his stone searching for something about the Bone Lord that exposed a weakness. But there was nothing. He already knew it. There wasn't a way.

He remembered something and looked back at the old man. He knew the old man was kneeling with his head down. He knew it through his stone, but, when he looked back, for some reason he chose to open his eyes and look at the old man. Somehow, the old man felt his gaze and raised his head to lock eyes. The old man nodded and smiled.

He smiled! That reminded Arthur of their conversation in the basement when the old man had tried to warn him about his stone.

His cursed stone.

***

Arthur could hear Shannon making her way up from the basement. He and Caitlin were snuggled up against Dad on the big leather couch in the living room. He could hear William's steady breathing as he lay atop Mom. He was fast asleep which was amazing since he had just been kidnapped by a giant bat from his bedroom window, but Mom and Dad brought him back. His parents would always protect them.

"Your turn, Budd," said Shannon with an overtired drawl.

He groaned as he extracted himself from the shared warmth of his family and made his way down the basement stairs to learn more about his stone. He left the door to the basement open, just in case, and felt the outside of his left pocket where he kept his stone. The familiar hard off-spherical shape comforted him.

"Hello?" he called out as he came to the bottom of the stairs.

"Over here," came the old man's voice. He was sitting on the landing of a plastic little tyke's swing set with his feet dangling onto the red slide. Somehow, it made the old man look very young and extremely old at the same time. Arthur looked at his dark brown shirt. It was pretty dirty. He figured he should keep note of wherever the man sat so that Mom could clean it up later. He was sure that if he smacked the old man on the back it would produce a puff of dust like when he clapped his hands together with an 'empty' Quaker Oats Banana Oatmeal packet at breakfast. And, now that he thought about it, he was hungry. His stomach's rumbling agreed with him.

"So what are you going to teach me about my stone? Are you going to help me use it better?"

"No," said the old man. "If it were possible, I would advise you to cast your stone away."

"Um . . . why?"

"You have chosen the cursed stone," said the old man. "Each stone is powerful and dangerous, but the stone you have chosen is debilitating. It will limit you in sinister ways if you let it. No, I will not teach you to use your stone. That you have figured out for yourself. I must teach you to *unlearn* how to use your stone or you will become damned."

Arthur considered this for a minute. He thought that Shannon's stone was fairly dangerous and Dad's stone was weird and kind of scary. But his stone was useful and helped him to do lots of crazy things, like climb up the back of the mountainous Screecher and keep perfect balance. Unless it was poisoning him somehow or would make him blind forever, he couldn't understand how it could be bad.

"I have the green one, you know," said Arthur.

"Yes, I know," said the old man.

"Will it make me blind if I use it too much?"

"In a way," answered the old man.

"In a blind way? I know that it makes me blind for as long as I use it after I let go. I must have been blind for almost an hour today. Will I stay blind if I use it too much?" asked Arthur.

"Not as you think. The stone will extract its price and you will not be able to see with your eyes for however long you use it. But that is not the curse of the stone," said the old man.

Arthur sat down on the hard-packed, off-white carpet they had in the basement. He was tired, and the old man wasn't making sense. He crossed his legs and leaned back on his hands. He worked his fingers into the tramped-down carpet.

"Okay, so what's the curse?" asked Arthur.

The old man considered him for a minute before answering. "Tell me, what does the stone do?"

"It shows me everything around me within a half-mile, and I can see absolutely everything about everything. It helps me fight people and balance and to know what is going to happen next," said Arthur.

"That is exactly the problem," said the old man.

"What? That it helps me?" asked Arthur.

"No. That you believe it shows you everything," said the old man.

"It does! When I held the stone outside, I knew how many worms there were, how many blades of grass, how many pregnant mice there were. I knew how many bricks were used to make our house and where there are holes in the roof. And I didn't even need to think about it! It was just there in my head," said Arthur.

Again, the old man considered Arthur like a man trying to figure out how to fold a map. "That is the curse of the stone. It has already blinded you."

"Yeah, it did for a while, but now I can see," said Arthur.

"I'm not talking about your eyes. You may be able to see now, but you have lost your vision." Arthur blinked at the old man. He sighed. "Tell me again. How have you used your stone?"

"Well, I use my stone by touching it, and then when I close my eyes I can kind of see everything around me. It shows me everything and then I figure out what to do based on what I see. Simple, really," answered Arthur.

"That is exactly the trap! The green stone is a sinister one. It has been used many times before and it has destroyed nearly all of its owners," said the old man, shaking his head.

"Were you one of them, because I don't understand what you are saying," said Arthur.

"The green stone operates by making you think that all that exists is what you can see. It blinds your *vision* by enhancing your sight. You touch the stone and it shows you all that exists, as you say. To you, it is providing a great service when in reality it is cutting you off from the infinite possibilities of reality. By showing you more of what is, you are becoming blind to what *could* be," said the old man.

Arthur thought about that. "I don't think that is what it does. When I see everything, I see lots of things to do and a lot of them I wouldn't have thought of if I hadn't used my stone."

"The stone is already starting to take you. Listen to yourself!" said the old man, sliding down the slide to sit in front of Arthur. "The stone has convinced you to limit yourself to that which you see before you."

Arthur still wasn't sure if he wasn't getting something or if the old man was crazy. He was leaning toward crazy. "Isn't that what we all do?"

"No! No!" said the old man. "It is important that you understand this if you are to survive the green stone. Our intentions create reality. It is not up to reality to create our intentions."

Arthur threw his hands up admitting defeat. "I don't get it."

The old man looked frustrated. He ran the fingers of his left hand through his mangy, dirty grey hair. Arthur made mental note to not to shake hands with the old man if it came down to it.

"Legos!" said the old man. "You play with Legos, correct?"

"Yes . . ." said Arthur slowly.

"How to you play with Legos?" asked the old man.

"I decide what I want to build and then I build it," said Arthur.

"Yes! Very good," said the old man. "And what if you couldn't find enough Legos?"

"Then I would change it or build something else," said Arthur.

"No. That is the green stone talking," said the old man.

"What? I'm not supposed to change what I want even though I don't have enough Legos?" asked Arthur. "That doesn't seem reasonable."

The old man clapped his hands in excitement, "Yes! Exactly! Be unreasonable. Do not lower your intention to fit what you see. Use the power of your intention to create a new reality."

"And . . . make Legos out of thin air?" asked Arthur.

"If your design requires more Legos, then more Legos is what you need, not a new design," said the old man. "Then your problem becomes not how to change your design, but how to get more Legos."

"But how do I get more Legos?" asked Arthur.

"Just so! Very good," said the old man. "What if there are no more Legos? What if you cannot think of a way to get Legos?"

"I think I just asked you that," said Arthur.

"And now I'm asking you," said the old man, folding his arms under his white scraggly beard.

"And I cannot change what I'm building?" asked Arthur.

"It is what your mind willed. Your intention, the design, cannot be compromised."

"Then I'm stuck. I cannot change my design and I don't know how to get more Legos. I'm stuck," said Arthur.

"Not stuck," said the old man. "You must have faith."

"That Legos will appear out of thin air?" asked Arthur.

"No. That is hope. Hoping for things to go differently is a lost cause. Having faith in yourself to do the necessary work to find a way is what is needed from you," said the old man.

"So, it's up to me to find the Legos. I guess I could borrow some from someone or buy more," said Arthur.

"Very good. Yes," said the old man.

"How does this have anything to do with the green stone?" asked Arthur.

"It is the danger of thinking you know everything, that reality is what it is and that is all there is," said the old man. "But there is so much more. There is the infinite potential of what could be, which is every bit as real as what is as long as you are willing to apply your intention to get it."

"I don't get it," said Arthur flatly.

"When you and your sister were fighting the giant guardian, at what point did you decide it was hopeless? At what point did you decide to give up?" asked the old man.

"Never," said Arthur.

"Okay," said the old man. "And at what point did your stone show you how to defeat the guardian?"

"It didn't," said Arthur.

"And yet you did defeat it?"

"Yes."

"So based on everything the stone showed you, your plight was hopeless and yet you fought on," said the old man. "That is faith. That is believing in the power of your intention despite what you see before you. That is imposing your will to change reality. Do not accept what is impossible. Your intention will define what is possible for you."

"I still don't see what the problem is with my stone. All it does is show me everything about what is around me. It is just knowledge. Is there something wrong with knowledge?"

"No. Knowledge in of itself is neither good nor bad until we apply it to some use. It is a tool. What is dangerous is when it becomes the *only* tool. Many, especially those with much knowledge, are seduced into believing it is the only tool in their work belt. You must learn to use all of your tools."

"What other tools are there? I only have five senses and they just telling me more about what is around me," said Arthur.

"What you must learn to use is your mind-sight, the ability to see how the world should be and shall be. The stone you possess will overwhelm your eyesight to the point where you may believe that it is all that exists. You must resist that temptation to see and accept the world only as it is and not as it could be. If you can see the invisible then you can achieve the *impossible*," said the old man.

"It sounds like you are telling me to do things that cannot be done," said Arthur, shrugging one shoulder.

"Most people look around themselves to see what can be done. That is the common path, the temptation of the green stone. The rare few decide what needs to be done, then change their environment to make it happen," said the old man.

Arthur wasn't sure what the old man meant, but he nodded his head and made some small comments amounting to 'thanks', then dragged his body up the basement stairs to tell Caitlin it was her turn.

***

Arthur opened his eyes and let go of the stone. Every other time he had done that he had been blind, but not this time. This time he could see.

He looked back at the old man who was still kneeling with his head bowed in respect to the Bone Lord. With his real eyes he saw him slightly nod his head. He knew what needed to be done. He didn't know how he would do it, but he knew it had to be done. That was all that mattered. He had to have faith.

Arthur left the stone in his pocket and turned back to the dais where the Bone Lord and inner circle were waiting for him to give his request.

His voice boomed throughout the cavern. "I challenge you, Bone Lord. *I* will become leader of the Grith."

END

ABOUT THE AUTHOR

Peter lives in the southern United States with his princess (wife) and four little monsters (the kids – yes, they are monsters). He is a trained wizard (PhD in Chemical Physics) and works as a blacksmith (metals industry). In his free time he enjoys adventuring with the monsters, escaping to faraway lands with his princess and performing feats of strength (amateur strongman competitions).

www.ingramcontent.com/pod-product-compliance
Lightning Source LLC
Chambersburg PA
CBHW062132170626
46813CB00002B/667